Sefton Libraries Bookface   @seftonLibraries   Sefton Libraries

Your library Sefton

Please return this item by the due date:

23 Feb 18

15. 8

WITHDRAWN FROM STOCK

Please return this item by the due date
or renew at **www.sefton.gov.uk/libraries**
or by telephone at **any** Sefton library:

Bootle Library   **0151 934 5781**
Crosby Library   **0151 257 6400**
Formby Library   **01704 874 177**
Meadows Library   **0151 288 6727**
Netherton Library   **0151 525 0607**
Southport Library   **0151 934 2118**

your Library Sefton

THE RUNAWAY
BRIDE AND THE
BILLIONAIRE

THE RUNAWAY BRIDE AND THE BILLIONAIRE

BY

KATE HARDY

First published in Great Britain 2017
By Mills & Boon, an imprint of HarperCollins*Publishers*
1 London Bridge Street, London, SE1 9GF

Large Print edition 2017

© 2017 Pamela Brooks

ISBN: 978-0-263-07171-9

This book is produced from independently certified FSC paper to ensure responsible forest management. For more information visit www.harpercollins.co.uk/green.

Printed and bound in Great Britain
by CPI Group (UK) Ltd, Croydon, CR0 4YY

To Liz Fielding, Scarlet Wilson
and Jessica Gilmore—
I thoroughly enjoyed our time creating
the Marlowe girls and Villa Rosa!

PROLOGUE

YOU WEREN'T SUPPOSED to be jealous of your twin. Especially when you knew she'd just been through a rough time and she deserved every bit of happiness. And *especially* when it was her wedding day.

Immi really hoped that Andie was feeling so loved-up with Cleve that her twin-sense was temporarily muted and she had no idea that one of her bridesmaids was having a serious wobble.

Though, actually, Immi had a feeling that all three of the bridesmaids were having a serious wobble right now. Posy, the baby of the family, had a smile so bright and brittle that it was practically cracking. The same was true of Portia, the oldest of the Marlowe girls: the family rebel who was behaving so perfectly that she might as well have 'faking it' written across her forehead in bright red lipstick.

Maybe she should suggest a midnight rendez-vous on the beach, where the three of them could sit and talk—just as they had when they'd been children, snuggling up beneath a duvet and having whispered conversations late into the night. Maybe they could help each other with their problems. But Posy seemed to have closed off to everyone since she'd joined the ballet corps and Portia wasn't given to talking about personal stuff.

And what did Immi have to whine about anyway? She had a job she loved, helping to run Marlowe Aviation, the family firm; and she was in the run-up to her wedding to Stephen Walters, who was all set to be promoted to her father's second-in-command at work.

Except Stephen didn't look at her the way that Cleve looked at Andie.

And Immi had a nasty feeling that she didn't look at him the way that Andie looked at Cleve:

as if there was nobody else on the surface of the planet.

She shook herself. It was probably just the stress of organising her own wedding making her so antsy. There were only two months to go and it had snowballed into a massive affair. Everything was completely under control—organising was what Immi did best—but now she'd seen how gorgeous her sister's quiet, understated wedding was, it brought home to her that the bridezilla stuff wasn't what she really wanted for herself, either.

The doubts had been creeping in for weeks. She'd overheard Stephen's best man Jamie saying that all he had to do was keep his nose clean until Imogen said 'I do' and he got the corner office. At the time, she'd tried to dismiss it as banter, but now she wondered if there was something more to it. Stephen had said he was too busy to take time off for Andie's wedding, and because it was only a small affair he was sure nobody would mind if he didn't make it. But was a man as ambitious as Stephen Walters really too busy to attend the wedding of the boss's daughter—his own fiancée's twin? Or did he have other reasons for not wanting to be here?

Oh, for pity's sake. She had to stop overthinking things.

And she really had to stop the paranoia. What had happened eight years ago wasn't going to repeat itself. So what if it was a cliché, marrying the boss's daughter? Stephen said he loved her. Wanting all the extra frills was just being selfish. Immi was done with being selfish. She'd put her family through enough worries. No more.

Imogen Marlowe looked amazing, Matt thought.

The first time he'd met her, she'd been wearing a power suit, all businesslike and slightly intimidating and determined to find out exactly what was going on with her twin. The second time he'd met her, early this morning, she'd been barefoot, wearing ankle-grazer faded jeans teamed with an oversized sweater, with a streak of mud on her face from where she'd been raiding the garden for flowers—the beautiful white marguerite daisies that she'd turned into raffia-tied bouquets for the bride and the bridesmaids, and the osteospermum that graced the tables in tin cans with an organza ribbon tied in a bow around them.

Right now, she looked the epitome of cool elegance in a teal-coloured vintage couture gown. The dress was sleeveless, with straps a finger width wide and a neckline that just skimmed her collarbones. A large round brooch made from tiny white seed pearls and four large black pearls was pinned on a vertical bow in the centre of the empire line bodice, and she wore a matching pearl collar. Her dark hair was cut in an immaculate, sharp bob and her make-up was discreet and understated.

And Matt really, really wanted to untie that bow and unwrap her from that dress. Find out exactly what that material was hiding.

He shook himself. Maybe it was the wedding

making him soppy. The best man and the bridesmaid, indeed.

But, as the best man, he *was* supposed to dance
with the bridesmaid.

At that very second, human speech seemed
to have deserted him. Which was crazy. What
was it about this woman that made him feel all
tongue-tied?

'That's a gorgeous dress, Imogen,' he said in
the end, knowing it sounded lame but not having a clue what else to say.

'Thank you. It's one of Sofia's—my sister Posy's godmother. And the amazing costume jewellery belonged to her too.' She gestured to the
brooch and the collar.

'I kind of guessed that.' He smiled. 'It's nice
that all four of you sisters are wearing one of her
dresses.'

'It's almost like her still being here with us,'
Immi agreed. 'I remember coming to the villa
as a child and Sofia always let us play dress-up
with her amazing clothes. Though I guess that

was because we always treated her stuff with respect—we didn't smear chocolate everywhere or rip things.' She smiled. 'I don't ever remember seeing this dress when I was little, but it's so stunning: like an eighteenth-century mantua dress, but updated to have a modern profile.'

'Mantua?' he asked.

She gestured to the bow. 'An open-fronted dress with a matching train and petticoat, and the train's lifted up to show the petticoat.'

'Mantua. I'll remember that.'

'I only know that because my guilty secret is watching historical dramas,' she said, giving him a rueful smile that made his heart feel as if it had done a backflip. 'Portia knows more about that stuff than I do, really.'

Portia was the Hollywood reporter, he remembered. The oldest sister.

'And it's good of Posy to let us all borrow the dresses and jewellery. Strictly speaking, they all belong to her now—along with the villa.'

'But sisters always share. At least, mine do,' he said.

'You have sisters?' She looked surprised.

'Four. All younger than me.'

'So you're used to all the talking, then.'

It was his turn for the rueful smile. 'Just a bit. Um, as the bridesmaid and the best man, I'm guessing we ought to…?'

'That would be lovely,' she said, and let him lead her onto the temporary dance floor.

This was bad, Immi thought. Seriously bad.

Matt Stark was Cleve's best man—a guy who lived in the cottage down the road and had kept an eye on the Villa Rosa since Sofia's death. According to Andie, he was a computer genius who'd made a fortune from a computer program that helped people run their homes by voice control—everything from turning a house alarm on or off to opening curtains, changing the thermostat on a heating system or dimming a light. Immi had been introduced to Matt's mother

Gloria earlier, and understood at that moment exactly what had driven her son to make the program: Gloria was in a wheelchair, crippled by arthritis, and Matt's computer system had given her back some of her independence.

He'd kept an eye on Sofia, too; although he hadn't managed to persuade her to let him install a satellite phone for emergencies, she had agreed to let him rig up a bell she could ring if she needed help.

And he'd rescued Immi's spider-hating twin from having to stick her head in a cupboard full of cobwebs.

Matt Stark was one of the good guys, and it was fine for her to like him instantly.

It was also fine for her to appreciate that he was good-looking—tall, with brown eyes and dark hair brushed back from his forehead, and a tiny little quirk at the corners of his mouth that told her he smiled often.

What *wasn't* fine was for her to tingle where he

touched her. Particularly because she didn't feel like that when her husband-to-be touched her.

She needed to get a grip. Make an excuse that she needed to go and fiddle with the flowers on the table, or something. But for the life of her she couldn't pull herself out of Matt's arms. It felt as if she was under some weird kind of spell. All the social graces she used every single day in business had simply deserted her. She had no idea what to say to him.

Worse still, she found herself looking at his mouth again. Wondering. Supposing it was just the two of them and the night and the music? Dancing under the stars, in the garden that over-looked the sea, with the air full of the scent of roses...

And he was looking at her mouth as if he was thinking exactly the same thing. Wondering what it would be like if they kissed. Wondering how she tasted.

She couldn't breathe.

This was all wrong. She shouldn't even be

thinking about kissing another man. She was getting married in eight weeks' time. She was meant to be in love with her fiancé, not thinking about kissing Matt Stark in front of her entire family at her twin sister's wedding.

And yet she could feel her lips parting. Feel him drawing her that tiny bit closer, enough that she could feel the heat of his body against hers. Feel herself tipping her head back...

Insta-lust, that was what his sisters called this feeling, Matt remembered. Instant crazy attraction.

It had nothing to do with the glamorous dress or the high heels, and everything to do with the woman in his arms. She felt soft and sweet and the perfect fit. And he was pretty sure she felt it, too: because her hazel eyes had turned almost golden, her pupils were huge and that perfect rosebud mouth was parted ever so slightly.

All he had to do was dip his head...

And he was just about to do it when he noticed something.

Something that made him feel as if several buckets of ice-cold water had been dropped on him.

How the hell had he missed that rock on her left hand? That huge hands-off-she's-mine signal?

It might be traditional for the best man to dance with the bridesmaid, but that was as far as this could go. Much as Matt wanted to kiss Imogen Marlowe, he couldn't. He didn't remember seeing her with anyone at the actual wedding, but that massive diamond practically screamed that she was engaged.

He forced himself to ask, 'Is your fiancé here this evening?'

And then he saw all the colour drain out of her face and horror fill her eyes. As if she were completely shocked by what had almost just happened.

'I—er, no. He couldn't make it. Business,' she said swiftly.

Business was more important than the wedding of his fiancée's twin sister?

If Immi had been his sister and her fiancé hadn't shown up to the wedding of any of the other sisters, Matt would've been asking some very serious questions. Starting with whether said fiancé was the right man for her, if he couldn't put her first in his life.

But this was none of his business.

And he wasn't going to get involved with someone who wasn't free.

'Pity,' Matt said, keeping his voice as expressionless as possible. And as soon as the dance was over, he gave her his politest smile. 'I guess I need to dance with the other bridesmaids now.'

'Best man duties. Of course,' she said, looking relieved.

'See you later.' And he'd make very sure that there was distance between them for the rest of the evening. No more up close and personal. Because Imogen Marlowe was completely off limits.

CHAPTER ONE

A month later

'HONEY, I'M HO—' Immi stopped mid-word in the entrance hall of her flat.

There were shoes lying in the middle of the floor, clearly kicked off and abandoned without a thought—women's shoes that weren't hers.

A little further on was a skirt. Also not hers.

A top. Also not hers.

A black lacy push-up bra, just outside the door to her bedroom.

She dragged in a breath. There had to be good reason for a trail of another woman's clothes leading to her bedroom. Stephen knew she wasn't due back from her business trip until tomorrow. Maybe he'd lent the key to the flat to one of his friends.

Because the logical explanation made her sick to her stomach.

Her fiancé wouldn't be cheating on her, in her own bed, a month before their wedding…would he?

But there were noises coming from the bedroom. Familiar noises. And the hope that she was making a fuss over nothing died as she heard a woman screaming, 'Oh, Stephen!'

Oh, God…oh, God…oh, God…

This was eight years ago, all over again. When she hadn't been feeling well at a party and had gone to get her coat from the bedroom, only to discover her boyfriend having sex under the pile of coats with another girl.

Except this time was so much worse. Because it wasn't the teenage boy she'd given her virginity to, the boy who'd sneered from under the pile of coats that he'd only slept with her for a bet because nobody would have really wanted to sleep with Immi the Elephant.

This was the man she was meant to be *marrying.*

Cold seeped all the way through her. There had to be some mistake.

'Oh, Stephen, yes!'

No mistake, then.

She dragged in a deep breath. She could back away, close the front door quietly, pretend she hadn't seen anything and then go to a coffee shop. Then she could call Stephen to say that she'd managed to conclude her meeting early and would be home in an hour. It would give him enough time to get his girlfriend out of her flat and clean up all traces of the woman's presence. Immi could simply forget what she'd seen and pretend that nothing had happened.

But did she really want to spend the rest of her life living a lie? Marry a man who clearly didn't love her, despite his protestations—because why else would he be seeing another woman behind her back?

Immi the Elephant.

She shook herself. She wasn't an insecure, unhappy teenager any more. And she wasn't going to do what she'd done back then and try to starve herself into what she'd thought was an acceptable shape. She'd worked hard to become who she was now: Imogen Marlowe, a strong, successful businesswoman.

And she was going to deal with this exactly as a strong, successful businesswoman would.

Lifting her chin, she marched over to the bedroom door. She banged on it twice—judging that it would give Stephen's girlfriend just about enough time to cover herself with bedding, because Immi definitely didn't need to be faced with the total naked truth—and opened the door.

'What the—?' Stephen began.

'Who the hell are you?' the girl squeaked, holding the bedclothes tightly against herself. 'Stevie? What's going on?'

Immi stared at the girl. She looked young, easily impressed. No doubt Stephen had turned on the charm. Charm that Immi now knew was as designer as his clothes and just as easily shed. 'I,' she said quietly, 'am the person who owns this flat. Stephen's fiancée.' She gave a tight smile. 'Well, I was his fiancée up until about two minutes ago, when I walked in to find your clothes all over the floor in my hallway and you screaming his name in my bed.'

The girl at least had the grace to blush and fall silent.

'Immi! Look, this isn't what you—' Stephen began.

'On the contrary,' Immi cut in. 'It's exactly what I think it is. And now I know what Jamie meant by keeping your nose clean until the wedding. Pity you didn't listen to him. But I'm glad you didn't—because if I'd come home early from business and caught you in my bed with a girlfriend after we were married, it would've been that much worse. At least now I don't have the mess of a divorce to deal with.' Just a big, glitzy wedding to unpick. A wedding that had already snowballed until it felt as if it had taken on a life of its own.

Stephen looked too shocked to say another word.

Good.

Because she was only just holding herself together as it was.

She took his engagement ring off her finger and dropped it on the floor. 'I'm going out for an hour and a half,' she said. 'When I get back, I expect you, your girlfriend and all your stuff to be gone.'

'But, Immi—'

'And you needn't bother returning your key or getting it back from however many women you've given it to,' she cut in, not wanting to hear any excuses, 'because I'm getting the locks changed.'

'Immi, don't do this. I love you.'

A month or so ago, she might have believed him. But not after her twin's wedding. Not after seeing the emotion in the eyes of a man who really did love the woman walking down the aisle towards him. 'No,' she said. 'You love the idea of being married to the boss's daughter. Getting the corner office.' And how it hurt to admit it. She'd been Immi the Elephant, the means to win a bet, to Shaun. She'd been the means to an end for Stephen. She'd spent her teen years battling the feeling of inadequacy, and even now she had days when the doubts swamped her—but she still knew she deserved better than this. 'I'm guessing Dad might not be too keen on that idea, now.'

He went white. 'Immi—'

If he'd said that he was sorry, she might've considered listening to him. But instead he'd tried to pull the wool over her eyes. Tried to lie his way out of it. Tried to tell her that finding him completely naked with another woman *in her own bed* wasn't what she thought it was.

Did he think she was that pathetic and needy, that she'd go ahead and marry a man who clearly had no respect for her?

'No,' she said, and turned on her heel and walked out.

A few minutes later, Immi was sitting in a quiet corner of a nearby coffee shop, without a clue how she'd managed to walk there or how she'd even ordered anything, but in front of her was an espresso and her phone.

The phone whose ringer she'd turned to silent, but every time Stephen's name flashed up on the screen she hit the 'ignore' button.

She ignored his texts, too.

Well, she'd seen them on her screen. Each one was increasingly desperate—no doubt as he re-alised that the glittering prize of Marlowe Aviation was slipping out of his grasp.

Immi, please.

Forgive me.

I don't know why I did it.

I love you.

No. He didn't love her at all. And he knew exactly why he'd slept with that girl: because he wanted to.

She couldn't forgive him for a betrayal like that.

Particularly as he still hadn't said the little five-letter word that might've made her talk to him. So clearly he wasn't sorry at all. Or maybe just sorry that he'd been caught.

She took a sip of the coffee. It didn't taste of anything, but she forced herself to drink it. She was *not* going back to being the bad twin, the one everyone worried about because she'd gone off the rails and starved herself as a teen—not quite far enough to need hospitalisation, but enough to need counselling. The girl whose family looked at her collarbones before they looked at her face, and who made a point of hugging her just to check for themselves that she wasn't any more slender than the last time they'd hugged her.

Though at the same time she couldn't blame them. If Andie, Portia or Posy had been the one who'd had anorexia, she would've been worried sick and done exactly the same. She knew they all did it out of love.

OK. She'd do this Immi-style. Super-organised. She'd make a list, and tick each item off as she did it.

1: Book a locksmith for two hours' time.
2: Tell her family that the wedding was off.
3: Work through the list of everything she'd arranged for the wedding so far and cancel the lot.

Oh, wait. First things first. She blocked Stephen from her phone. At least then she could make her call to the locksmith in peace.

That was the easy one.

Now for the tough one. How did you tell your family that your wedding was off? They'd all want to know why. It made her squirm in her seat. Not only was she the cliché, engaged to her father's second-in-command, she was the one who'd been cheated on. It made her feel grubby. Stupid. She'd thought she'd made a safe choice of partner, a man her father approved of. She'd thought that Stephen would never treat her the way Shaun had. But she'd ended up hurt, just the same.

Maybe she'd wait for a couple of hours until she could think of the right words. The last thing she wanted was for everyone to rush back from their corners of the world: Andie from Kent, where she was settling in to married life and pregnancy with the man she loved more than anyone on earth and who loved her all the way back, Portia from LA, Posy from wherever she was dancing with the ballet corps—she was being even more elusive than usual—and her parents from their 'gap year' in India.

She could do this.

Though she still hadn't found the right words by the time she got back to her flat. As she'd half feared, Stephen was still there.

'Immi! Oh, thank God. I was so worried about you.'

Did he really expect her to believe that?

'You didn't answer any of my calls or my messages.'

Obviously. And he hadn't taken the hint—or her explicit request that he should leave before she got back.

'I asked you to leave,' she reminded him.

'I couldn't—not until we'd talked. Immi, it was a mistake.'

She took a step back before he could sweep her into his arms. She didn't want him to hold her and try to make her feel better. He was the reason she felt bad in the first place. And he'd made the choice. Even if the other woman had come on to him, he could've said no. Could've stayed faithful. Could've told her that he was flattered but he was getting married next month and wouldn't cheat on his fiancée.

He'd chosen to do the opposite.

'It doesn't have to be over,' Stephen said, his eyes beseeching.

How easy it would be for her to agree. Then she wouldn't have to unpick the wedding.

Wouldn't have to feel as if she'd let everyone down. Wouldn't have to face her family knowing what a naive, stupid fool she'd been, thinking that the man she loved felt exactly the same way about her.

But Immi looked at Stephen now and realised that, actually, she didn't love him any more. She'd thought maybe she was having an attack of cold feet at Andie's wedding: but it had been more like a wake-up call. If she married this man now, she knew she'd spend the rest of her life wondering if he was making another 'mistake' he expected her to forgive. Every time either of them went away on business, every time she visited her sisters on her own because he was 'too busy' to make it, would there be another woman keeping her place warm in his bed?

'Was she the first?' Immi asked.

Stephen looked shocked. 'How do you mean?'

Was he really going to be evasive, even now? 'I need you to be honest with me,' she said evenly. 'Was that girl the first time you'd cheated on me?'

He looked away, and she knew the truth. 'So that's what Jamie meant about keeping your nose clean.'

He blinked. 'How do you know about that?'

'I overheard.'

He frowned. 'You didn't say anything.'

'Because I thought I was overreacting. That I was tired. That I was letting the stress of the wedding get to me.' She paused. 'Were you with *her* when I was at Andie's wedding?'

'No.'

She didn't think he was lying. But she needed to know the whole truth, not just part of it. 'Were you with someone else?'

'It was a—'

'—mistake,' she finished for him, feeling sick. So that was at least two women he'd cheated with. How many others had there been? 'I don't want a marriage based on a mistake.'

'Immi, we're good together.'

She took another step backwards when he reached for her. 'No, we're not. If I was enough for you, you wouldn't be looking elsewhere.'

His skin turned a dull red. 'I guess.'

He'd been honest with her. Maybe she should be honest with him—and herself. 'And you're not enough for me.'

He stared at her. 'You what? Are you telling me there's been someone else for you, too?'

'No. Because I've never cheated on you.' That almost-kiss at Andie's wedding hadn't been cheating, because Immi hadn't actually done it. She'd thought about it, though, which was almost as bad in her view and it made her feel guilty.

'It's over, Stephen,' she said. 'I can't trust you, and I don't want a marriage that's full of suspicion and lies.'

'But—' He stared at her, looking horrified. 'We're getting married in a month.'

'Maybe you should've thought about that before you brought that girl home. To my bed.' Immi dug her nails into her palms. 'I can't marry you. But I'll deal with cancelling the wedding.' Because then at least she would know everything had been done properly. Stephen had completely undermined her trust in him. Maybe she was being a control freak, but she'd rather know that things had been cancelled instead of skipped over.

'What are you going to tell your parents?'

Good question. She still wasn't sure. 'I'll tell them the wedding's off.'

'So I've lost my job.'

Why did she feel that that upset him more than losing his wife-to-be? 'I don't know if Dad will sack you.' Paul Marlowe would probably want to sack Stephen—but whether he could actually do it in legal terms, Immi didn't know. Besides, surely any decent person would offer to resign? She didn't think her respect for Stephen could've withered any more, but apparently it just had. 'Dad isn't here.' And Stephen, as his temporary second-in-command, would hardly sack himself. 'I'll be speaking to Priya in HR, but I guess it's going to be awkward in the office tomorrow.' She paused. 'Unless you maybe call in sick.'

'And then get sacked for lying?' he scoffed. 'Hardly.'

So, even though he was completely in the wrong, he wasn't going to make this easy for her? 'Your choice,' she said. She couldn't do anything about the work situation, but she could at least do something about the home situation. And this was her flat, not theirs. He hadn't paid a penny towards the mortgage and he couldn't claim any rights in it. 'Did you pack your stuff?'

'No.'

Clearly he'd expected to talk her round. He'd got that one wrong, too. Something else to add to her list, then. 'Go and stay with Jamie. I'll have your stuff delivered to his place.'

'Immi, it doesn't have to be this way,' he said urgently. 'We can get through this.'

'No, we can't,' she said. She'd never told him about Shaun's betrayal, and she wasn't going to tell him now. But she'd never, ever trust him again. Personally or professionally. 'I'm not going to change my mind. The wedding's off. Please just go, Stephen.'

For a moment, she thought he was going to argue with her. But then, to her relief, he left without a fight.

As she double-locked the door behind him, she realised that he still hadn't said sorry.

And that was somehow the saddest thing.

She was halfway through composing a text to her family when her phone beeped.

The message was from Andie.

You OK? Xxx

Twin-sense again.

I'm fine.

She wasn't quite sure if it was true or not, right at that moment, but she knew she would be fine. She'd get through this.

Have news. Telling everyone at same time. Give me five minutes. xxx

Please, don't let her twin think that Immi was playing catch-up again and following in her footsteps with news about a baby. That wasn't happening any time soon. If ever. Not that she'd ever discussed any of that with her family.

And now she definitely had to tell her family about her broken engagement. She had less than five minutes.

There wasn't a way to break the news gently. She blew out a breath and typed the bald statement.

Am calling off the wedding.

If she told them why, all hell would break loose. Then again, if she didn't tell them why, all hell would break loose. Better to tell the truth.

Stephen has met someone else.

Though she didn't have to tell them quite how she'd found out, did she?

I'm fine. Don't worry. But I don't want to talk to anyone right now, OK?

No way would her family respect that. But she wanted to allay the fears she knew they'd all have straight away. The fears they'd always have, thanks to her teenage years: anorexia was a mental illness with physical symptoms, and of course they'd worry that she'd relapse. Even though she'd spent quite a while in counselling and worked hard to overcome her problems.

PS I *am* eating. Don't worry.

She ended with a smiley face she didn't feel. And three kisses.
Then she added a second text to her parents.

Please do *not* rush home from India. All is under control. Or it will be. See you next month. Love you! xxx

Then she called their HR manager. 'Priya, I'm so sorry to call you outside work, but we've got a bit of a tricky situation.' She explained what had happened.

'What a bastard,' Priya said, sounding outraged. 'I can't believe he did that to you. Are you all right?'

'I will be,' Immi said. 'I was kind of hoping he'd offer to resign.'

'But he's too selfish for that.' Priya sighed. 'What he did was despicable—but it's to do with his personal life outside work. So, much as I'd like to sack him, I can't. I can't even give him a written warning or put him on gardening leave.'

'Dad will probably want to kick him out.'

'And then Stephen could take him to a tribunal and make a claim for unfair dismissal.' Priya paused. 'Do you think it's likely that he can do any damage to the business?'

Would he really turn out to be that nasty, and try to damage the business now his ambitions had been thwarted? 'I guess anything he does will leave either a paper trail or an electronic trail that would lead straight back to him. If he's determined to stay then I don't think he's stupid enough to do anything where Dad could sue him for misconduct or negligence.'

'Do you want to move your desk to my office first thing, so you don't have to face him?' Priya offered.

'You are the world's biggest sweetheart,' Immi said, 'and I really appreciate the offer, but no. I'm not letting him drive me out of my office. Maybe seeing me every day will make him feel guilty enough to do the right thing and leave.'

'Once people know what he's done—and it won't be from me,' Priya said, 'I have a feeling that nobody in Marlowe Aviation is going to talk to him ever again.'

'It's a mess,' Immi said. 'But I'm going to stick it out. I'm not letting him drive me out of my family's business.'

'Good,' Priya said. 'And my door is open any time you need it, OK?'

'Thanks.'

When she'd finished the call, she saw she had a screen full of texts.

Get that you don't want to talk, her twin said, but do you need a hand unpicking the wedding?

Typical Andie, being practical.

Immi texted back.

Thanks, but am fine.

And she was surprisingly fine. It felt as if a huge weight had just been lifted from her shoulders—which in itself told her that cancelling the wedding had been the right thing to do. Marrying Stephen would've been a huge, huge mistake.

Will let you know if I get stuck on anything.

There was one from Posy.

Love you, let me know if you need anything. Portia's been at the villa. Go there if you need a break. xxx

Thanks. Might take you up on that later. Love you, too xxx, she texted back to Posy.

Getting the next flight home. Will sack him first thing in the morning, was her father's response.

This one she definitely had to handle in person. Sighing, she called her father's mobile. 'Dad?'

'How dare he hurt you like that? Who the hell does he think he is?' Paul Marlowe raged.

'Dad, I'm fine,' she said. 'And you can't sack him. I've already spoken to Priya. If you sack him, he can sue you for unfair dismissal.'

'What—after what he's done? That's totally unacceptable.'

'It's the law,' she said gently. 'Dad, really. It's fine. I'll manage. Don't cut your trip short. You're not supposed to be home until next month.' Which should've been for her wedding, but that wasn't going to happen now. 'You and Mum have planned this trip for ever and I don't want you missing out. It's fine.'

'Hmm,' Paul said. 'Your mother wants to speak to you.'

There was a brief pause, and then she heard her mother say, 'Are you all right, Immi?'

'I'm fine,' Immi said.

'Are you sure?'

'Yes. Actually, Stephen's probably done us both a favour. When Andie got married, I realised that he doesn't look at me the way Cleve looks at Andie, and I don't look at him the way Andie looks at Cleve. I thought maybe I was just having cold feet, but...'

'If it isn't right, it isn't right.'

But Immi could hear the worry in her mother's voice. 'Mum, I'm eating,' she said gently. 'I promise, I'm not going to start starving myself. I'm older now and much, much wiser. Do you want me to video myself eating every meal and send you the evidence?'

'Yes,' Julie said. 'Well, obviously that'd be a bit excessive. But I'm your mother. I wouldn't be human if I didn't worry about you. I let you down last time.'

'No, you didn't. I was a teenager, and teenagers

are very good at hiding things we don't want our parents to know. Honestly. I'm eight years older than I was back then, and the counselling really sorted me out. My head's in a good place. Yes, I'm angry and hurt, and I might tape Stephen's picture on a punchbag at the gym and pound it to shreds, but that's as far as it'll go. Don't worry. I really want you and Dad to finish your trip.'

'I should be home, helping you cancel all the wedding stuff.'

'It's fine. I have lists. Andie's already offered to help. It'll be fine,' Immi soothed.

'But you'll ring me if you need me?'

'I'll ring you,' Immi promised. 'But you and Dad have been looking forward to India. Just go to all the places and take a gazillion photos to show me when you get home. Love you, Mum.'

'Love you, too,' Julie said.

Immi had just finished packing the last of Stephen's stuff into a box when her phone beeped again. This time it was Portia.

OMG. When did this happen? Want me to come home and scalp him?

Immi laughed and texted back,

Tonight. I'm fine. Going to tape his pic to punchbag at gym tomorrow. You OK?

Yes.

Good.

Need a hand with cancelling stuff?

No, I've got it. But thanks.

Right at that moment, Immi really missed her sisters and she would've liked nothing better than to spend an evening with the four of them curled up by the fire with mugs of hot chocolate and a plate of brownies, talking about nothing in particular. But her sisters all had busy lives. And she wasn't going to drag everyone back to Cambridge just because her own life was taking a bit of a wobble.

See you soon, yes?

Laters, Portia texted back.

So that was the first hurdle dealt with, Immi thought. Now she needed to put her list together of people she needed to call to cancel the ceremony, the reception, the dresses and the flowers, the photographer… And she might just take her little sister up on her offer of a bolt hole in a month's time. Facing everyone this week would be tough enough, but the week when she was supposed to have been married? That was the week she'd rather be as far away from here as possible.

And in the meantime she had work to do.

CHAPTER TWO

A month later

IMMI PAID THE taxi driver, thanked him and collected her bags from the back of the car.

The Villa Rosa loomed before her in all its
pink faded glory.

The last time she'd come here to L'Isola dei
Fiori had been for Andie's wedding. When she'd
still been engaged to Stephen...while he'd been
seeing someone else behind her back.

She shook herself. Enough of the pity party. It
was bad enough that she was behaving like the
Runaway Bride—actually running away from
things on the week she should've been getting
married. But she really couldn't bear to be in
Cambridge facing everyone's pity right now;
plus her father was back at the helm of Mar-

lowe Aviation, so it wasn't as if she was letting him down. And she really needed time away from the whole situation to decide what she really wanted from life.

Thank God Posy's godmother Sofia had left her this place. It had been a gift to Sofia years ago by her besotted lover Ludano, the King of L'Isola dei Fiori; and Sofia had bequeathed it to her goddaughter, the youngest Marlowe girl.

OK, so the house needed some work doing. A lot of work, Immi amended, given that the stucco was faded and there were even weeds growing out of a crack in the wall. But it had been a bolt hole that all of Posy's sisters had needed this spring and summer. Andie, giving her time to come to terms with a life-changing event. Portia, when her career was teetering on the brink. And now Immi herself, giving her space to decide what she was going to do with her life now her marriage wasn't happening.

Best of all, the garden here had run pretty much wild. Which meant that Immi could spend her days doing what she loved second-best in the whole world—working in a garden—and it would make her so physically tired that she wouldn't be able to brood about the might-have-beens. She could just concentrate on the plants and let a few ideas bubble in her subconscious.

The keys were right where Posy said they'd be, underneath a flowerpot in the back garden, and she let herself in.

The house was clean—as Immi had expected, given that her older sister Portia had been staying here—and there had definitely been some work done: the cracked glass panels in the double-height conservatory had been replaced, meaning that the room was pretty much watertight again. Several other walls had been replastered, though not painted, and the once-gorgeous painted drawing room still had a crack running through the fresco; it had been repaired, but nobody had touched up the paint.

She hauled her bags into the kitchen. Just as she remembered from the weekend of the wedding, the room was large and comfortable, and she thought she could probably use it as her base. The oven was ancient but in working order, as was the fridge. The kettle sitting on the worktop was the kind you had to boil on top of the stove, rather than the electric kind with a light that switched off when the water had boiled, but again it was workable; the pans, although worn and not the non-stick kind she was used to, were serviceable enough. The place felt as if it had been stuck in the early nineteen-seventies, but it had a certain charm.

There was a note propped against the kettle; she picked it up and read it.

Posy said you were coming. Have put milk in fridge and bread in the cupboard. We're in the white cottage down the lane if you need anything.
Matt Stark

Matt.
Immi remembered that almost-kiss at the wedding and caught her breath. Back then, she hadn't

been free to act on that unexpected and unfair surge of desire. Now she was. Though right now she wasn't in a place where she wanted to get involved with anyone. Just let it go and chalk it up to the actions of a kind neighbour, she told herself.

And it *was* kind of Matt to have brought her some milk and bread. She'd planned to go shopping once she got here, but her flight had been delayed and she'd missed her original ferry crossing from the mainland to Sant'Angelo, meaning that she'd arrived at the villa much later than she'd intended. She knew the shops in the village would be closed now; hopefully Portia had left some cereal or something in one of the cupboards, but if not then toast and milk would see her through until tomorrow. She'd call in and thank Matt for his kindness in the morning.

But how good it was right now not to have to talk to anyone.

It felt as if she'd spent the last month doing nothing but talking, cancelling every single thing she'd arranged for the wedding and uninviting all the guests. Everyone had wanted to know why the wedding was off. She'd squirmed at the idea of telling people the truth, not wanting to have to face all the pity; but not telling the truth left her open to all the gossip and speculation, and even the blame—flighty Imogen Marlowe changing her mind and cancelling the wedding at the last minute, leaving poor Stephen devastated.

Ha. The only flying she was doing was in aeroplanes; and Stephen wasn't devastated at losing her. He was devastated at losing his chance to run Marlowe Aviation.

She'd fudged her way through it, simply saying that Stephen had let her down badly over a really important issue, and the marriage would've failed. Better to call it off now than to go through with it and then end up with a messy divorce.

Work had been harder.

Facing him, every single day, had been tough. The first few days, Stephen had started trying to charm her round, bringing her fresh flowers for her desk every day. When she hadn't given in, he'd moved on to blaming her for his behaviour, saying that he'd only strayed because she hadn't been enough for him. Words that had cut deep because they'd brought back her old teenage fears of being inadequate. He'd probably said it just to hurt her when she'd refused to take him back, but the barb had landed on target. She'd been close to punching him, but she wasn't going to give him the satisfaction of slapping her with an assault charge.

The blaming had been followed by a week of sneers and nasty little digs. Immi had managed to ignore them, for the most part, but when he pushed her to almost her breaking point she'd asked Priya to send him a formal letter about standards of professional behaviour in the office. He'd backed off after that.

But then there had been a week of fielding the tension between her father and Stephen, once Paul and Julie Marlowe had returned from their extended trip to India. Immi had had to try to stop her father going off at the deep end and leaving himself open to having to pay Stephen massive compensation at an industrial tribunal—because having to pay compensation to the man who'd cheated on her would've really added insult to injury.

Being away from that whole toxic situation was bliss; and, even though she still worried that her father would lose his temper, Immi knew that Priya would sit him down and talk him through the legal issues. With Priya not being his daughter, there was a chance that Paul Marlowe might actually listen to her.

A few days here on L'Isola dei Fiori, on her own, and she might be able to work out exactly where she went from here. What she was going to do with the rest of her life. With no internet—and spotty mobile phone reception only on some parts of the island, if she was lucky—she wouldn't have to answer any questions until she was ready. Though it might be an idea to take selfies of herself eating and send them to her sisters and her mother, just to reassure everyone that she wasn't slipping back into her old ways. She'd need to wait until tomorrow, when she had a little more than just bread and milk in the cupboard.

To her relief, Portia had left decent instant coffee and hot chocolate.

Immi made herself a mug of coffee, unpacked her stuff in Sofia's faded yet comfortable downstairs bedroom, then headed for the garden with a notebook and pen so she could walk round and start making a list of what needed doing and where.

Alberto, Sofia's old gardener, was too old and frail now to keep everything under control. According to Andie, one of his and Elena the housekeeper's sons cut the grass every spring, and it didn't tend to grow much during the summer. The shrubs and the roses, however, were well out of control, overgrown and with whippy stems that could catch the unwary and draw blood. It was just as well that she'd brought her own secateurs and gardening gloves from home, and she might need something even sturdier than that to tackle the thicker stems. Hopefully there was a saw or something in the garage.

She found an ancient and slightly rusted wheelbarrow in the garden shed, and hauled it over to the border nearest the house. Might as well get a bit of weeding in; and then tomorrow she'd put her list in order and start working her way through cutting back the tangle.

The physical work did her good; by the time she'd spent a couple of hours weeding, she was tired and ached all over.

Bath and an early night, she decided. She made herself some toast, then waited for the massive bath to fill. Back in the day, this must've been really special, she thought. Now, the bath had patches where the enamel had worn away, and several of the sumptuous peacock-blue-and-gold tiles had cracked. The grouting was nothing short of horrible, and no amount of scrubbing was going to fix it. Some of the black-and-white-chequered lino had cracked. The whole place was going to need a lot of love to bring it back to its former glory—and probably more money than she, Posy, Portia and Andie had between them.

Unless maybe Portia could use some of her contacts to get a television programme made about the restoration, with experts and tradesmen giving their time and labour in return for the national or even international exposure on TV... Immi made a note on her phone to suggest it to Portia, then stepped into the bath and scrubbed herself clean.

Without a shower, she'd had to use a jug from the kitchen to rinse the shampoo from her hair; she tucked a towel sarong-style around herself and wrapped her wet hair in a smaller towel before going back to Sofia's bedroom, where she tripped over something and pitched head-first onto the bed.

'Way to go, Immi,' she said, rolling her eyes, and got back onto her feet. She could hear a bell clanging somewhere, and assumed it was the church in the village. Maybe that was somewhere to explore tomorrow.

She changed into her pyjamas and combed her hair, then headed for the kitchen to make herself a mug of hot chocolate. But as she reached the doorway she could see torchlight flashing. For a second, she froze. Was it a burglar? There was nothing here to steal. Sofia's jewellery was gorgeous, but it was all costume and not worth anywhere near what the value would've been if it had been real.

All the same, she couldn't let the house be ransacked. She ran into the kitchen and snatched up the first thing to hand, then yelled, *'Va via! Ho chiamato la polizia!'*

Hopefully the burglars wouldn't know she had no landline and no signal for her mobile phone, and would believe that she really had called the police. And hopefully they'd make a run for it.

To her shock, the kitchen light was slammed on. She shrieked and was about to whack the burglar with the saucepan she was holding, when she suddenly recognised him.

Matt Stark.

She blew out a breath and put the saucepan down on the nearest worktop. 'You scared me.'

'I'm sorry,' he said, his dark eyes filled with sincerity, 'but you rang the bell. I assumed you needed help.'

'I thought you were a burglar,' she said, and then his words sank in. 'Rang the bell? What bell?'

'There's a cord fixed by Sofia's bed and in the living room by her chair,' he explained. 'Her phone line came down several years ago and has never been fixed.'

Probably, Immi thought, after Ludano's death Sofia had no longer had any access to the palace staff to fix any problems. And Posy's godmother had been too proud to admit that she couldn't afford to fix the phone line.

'And she wouldn't let me rig up any kind of satellite phone for her,' he continued, 'so we compromised on her ringing a bell if she needed me.'

'I didn't pull any cord,' she said, and then wrinkled her nose. 'Oh. That's what I must've tripped over. And I did hear a bell—I just didn't connect it with tripping over. I thought it was the village church.'

'Well, now you know,' he said.

Her skin prickled with awareness—of him, and of the fact that she was only wearing thin cotton pyjamas that didn't exactly hide her shape. She sucked in a breath. She needed to calm herself down. Remembering her manners would be a good start. 'Thank you for the bread and the milk,' she said. 'I was going to call in tomorrow to say thank you and give you the money for it.'

'There's no need. I think I can afford to buy a neighbour a couple of pints of milk and a load of bread.' He paused. 'So why were you tackling what you thought were burglars on your own?'

She looked at the saucepan she'd just put down.

'That wasn't going to be much use against a determined intruder, was it?'

'Hardly,' he said dryly.

Imogen looked amazing in those pyjamas. The soft strappy top revealed her curves, and although her shorts were demure enough he could see just how long her legs were. And Matt really had to remind himself that she was off limits.

'So why wasn't your fiancé tackling the burglars?' he asked. It was like a scab he couldn't stop picking at.

'He's not here.' She took a deep breath. 'And he's not my fiancé any more.'

She was free?

But the split must've been recent. He'd seen her only two months before, with that massive rock on her left hand. Had she been the one to instigate the break-up, or had her fiancé called off the engagement? Right now Matt knew he needed to tread carefully. 'I'm sorry.'

'I'm not.' She lifted her chin. 'Marrying Stephen would've been the biggest mistake ever.'

'So you called it off?'

She spread her hands. 'Some people would say that was enough to make me the Runaway Bride.'

He somehow didn't think that Imogen Marlowe would run away from anything. There was a lot more to this than she was telling.

Not that it was any of his business. And he didn't need to get involved. 'Well, if you're not being attacked by burglars, I guess I'd better leave you be,' he said.

'Or,' she said, 'I could put some proper clothes on and make you a cup of hot chocolate.'

Why on earth had she said that?

Wasn't the whole point of her stay in L'Isola dei Fiori to be on her own, and to think about her future without having to talk to a single person? Why was she asking Matt to stay? This was particularly stupid of her, given that almost-kiss at Andie's wedding reception. This was playing with fire.

His expression was unreadable. Then he nodded. 'You're probably wearing more right now than the average tourist would on the beach, but I'll make the hot chocolate while you get changed.'

'Deal. The hot chocolate's in the top cupboard to the right of the stove, the milk's where you put it, and the pan...' She smiled. 'Well. Let's just say it hasn't been used to smack a would-be burglar round the head.'

'Indeed.'

He smiled back, and all of a sudden she was covered in goosebumps. Which was ridiculous. For pity's sake, she was nearly twenty-five, not fifteen. She shouldn't be flustered just because a seriously attractive man smiled at her.

She went upstairs and changed into a clean T-shirt and jeans. When she came back down into the kitchen, the milk was just on the boil. Matt stirred the milk into the hot chocolate powder, then handed one of the mugs to her.

'There's a good spot in the garden,' he said, 'to look at the stars. Because there are so few homes on this part of the island there's hardly any light pollution so you get an excellent view of the night sky.'

'Sounds good to me,' she said. She'd been too busy around Andie's wedding—and too miserable—to notice the stars.

She slipped on a pair of canvas shoes but didn't bother lacing them up, then followed him and his torchlight out through the garden. The path wound through more of the overgrown shrubs, and a couple of times she started to wonder if this fabulous viewpoint of his even existed. She certainly didn't remember it from her childhood stays here. Wouldn't it have been easier just to sit on the ancient pink rocking chair she'd noticed on the terrace? But Matt seemed completely sure-footed, and eventually she found herself next to an old wooden bench in front of the wall that ran round the edge of the garden.

'I know it looks as if it'd be more sensible to just follow the wall,' he said, 'but the tremor a couple of years back caused the wall to crumble in places, so it's not brilliantly safe. Especially when it's not daylight, when you can't see where you're going and you're less likely to avoid tripping over a branch and going over the edge.'

'Right.' She knew the island was on a volcanic ridge. A tremor explained the cracks in the house; and they probably hadn't been fixed for the same reason as the phone line. 'I'm assuming the house needed attention before the wall round the garden did.'

He nodded. 'Cleve's done a bit of repairing—well, after almost burning down the kitchen—and when Javier was here with Portia he fixed the glass in the conservatory and plastered some of the walls.'

Immi had known Cleve for years and wasn't surprised that he was good with his hands, but she couldn't quite get her head round the idea of a movie star doing building work. Particularly as, from what she'd seen, the job looked pretty professional. But Portia had kept a lot of things about her new husband quiet, including the wedding: it was the only way to get real privacy when one of you lived so much in the public eye.

As Matt had promised, the bench that was perched on the edge of the cliff, facing out to sea, provided an expansive view of the star-filled sky and it was utterly beautiful.

It was a relief that he didn't fill the silence with small talk, either; they just sat there together in companionable silence, sipping hot chocolate and watching the stars twinkling brightly above.

'Thank you,' she said quietly. 'I think I needed that.'

'Time and space to think?' he asked, his voice equally soft.

'Yes. I'm pretty much at a crossroads in my life right now.' She wrinkled her nose. 'The plan is to sort out the garden here; if you're having to concentrate on physical work, you're giving your subconscious time to deal with the problem.'

'It's a plan,' he said.

'It sounds as if you don't think it's a good one.'

He lifted both hands in a gesture of surrender. 'No judgements. I'm doing the same kind of thing myself right now.'

There was something like sadness in his dark eyes and she wondered why he was at a crossroads. Though it was none of her business and it felt too intrusive to ask. 'Maybe I ought to paint the walls instead of tackling the garden,' she said. 'I'll have to talk to Posy about paint.'

'Are you good at painting?' he asked.

'I'm better at pruning,' she admitted.

'Then do the garden,' he advised. 'If you need space to think in the back of your head, it's easier to do it while you're doing something you love.'

What did he do when he needed to think? she wondered. Again, she felt too awkward to ask. Which was weird, because normally she got on well with people and never had a problem chatting to them.

But she knew what it felt like to be stuck.

And he'd been kind to her sisters and to Sofia. Time for payback. Maybe she could help him. 'I'm normally good at sorting things out,' she said, 'so if you want a non-judgemental neighbour to bounce ideas off...'

'Someone who doesn't know me and is outside the situation so might see it more clearly? I like that. Thank you.' He paused. 'I'm pretty good at sorting things out usually, too. So if you want...' He left the offer hanging open.

'Thanks, but it's a pretty tangled web.'

'They're the sort that could do most with an outside viewpoint.'

'I guess.' She paused. She could tell him what had happened. And that might put enough of a barrier between them to stop her doing something stupid. Like giving in to the pull she felt towards him. Or maybe it wouldn't. 'But maybe not today?'

'Any time,' Matt said. 'And you've had a day travelling. You must be tired. I'll let you get on.'

'Thanks.' She looked at him. 'How did you know about this bench, anyway?'

'It's where I always come to watch the stars,' he said. 'Sofia used to let me come here as a way of saying thanks for keeping an eye out for her.'

'Fair enough. I'm not going to interfere with that.' It wasn't her place in any case; the house belonged to Posy. Though Immi was pretty sure that her sister would be more than happy to let her neighbour come and look at the stars in her garden in exchange for keeping an eye on the place.

'I'll let you know if I'm here, so you don't think I'm a burglar.'

She thought about earlier when she'd intended to tackle him with a saucepan, wearing only pyjamas, and her skin heated. 'Indeed,' she said crisply, hoping that her voice didn't betray any of her confusion.

'I'll walk you back to the house,' he said.

She didn't really need protecting—but then again she didn't know the layout of the grounds that well, and he'd said that some of the walls on the edge of the cliff were crumbling. It'd be stupid to cut off her nose to spite her face. 'Thank you,' she said.

Once, twice, her hand brushed against his and, even though it was the lightest of contacts, it made her skin tingle. She tried to just tell herself that it was the location: Sofia's rambling, overgrown garden, smelling strongly of roses, under bright Mediterranean stars. But she knew it was more than that: and she was going to have to keep herself under very strict control when Matt was around. She wasn't in a place to start a relationship, and from the little he'd told her neither was he. They couldn't be anything more than just neighbours, acquaintances. Anything more would be unfair to both of them.

'Thanks for seeing me back,' she said when they reached the back door.

'Pleasure.' His dark, dark eyes were unreadable in the moonlight. 'You know where we are if you need anything.'

'Thanks.'

'And there's always the bell. The cord's by Sofia's bed and her chair,' he said.

Bed.

Definitely a word she shouldn't be thinking about around Matt Stark. Not if she wanted to keep her sanity.

'Thank you,' she said again. 'Goodnight.'

'Goodnight,' he said, and strode off towards the front of the house.

CHAPTER THREE

THE NEXT MORNING, Imogen was up early and thoroughly enjoyed having a cup of coffee and toast on the terrace, overlooking the garden and the sea. One definite change she'd make when she got back to England, she decided, would be to sell her flat and buy somewhere with a garden. The scent of the flowers here and the sound of the birds singing really were balm to the soul; although she'd looked after her parents' garden while they'd been away in their belated 'gap year', she wanted a proper garden of her own. The window boxes of her flat weren't enough.

Today she needed to get supplies. She had no idea what time the shops in the village opened, but late morning would be a fairly safe bet. And she wanted to take some flowers to Gloria,

Matt's mum, to thank her for the bread and milk. She really ought to take something for Matt, but in her experience very few men appreciated cut flowers, and she guessed that if he used herbs in cooking then he'd already have plants in his own garden. Maybe she could find something in the village.

She spent most of the morning weeding, then cut a bunch of white marguerite daisies—the ones she'd used in Andie's hair and for the bouquets at the wedding—for Gloria and tidied herself up, checking in the mirror that she didn't still have smudges of dirt on her face.

Carrying the flowers in an ancient wicker basket she'd found in one of the cupboards, she headed down the hill to the village. As she got halfway down the hill, her phone came into range of a signal and started beeping.

As she'd half expected, there was a barrage of texts from her sisters and her mother, plus one from Priya to say that she was managing to keep the peace in the office and not to worry about rushing back. She smiled and had replied to all of them by the time she got into the village.

The main square held the *alimentari*, a baker's and a butcher's shop. She paused to read the signs on the doors and made a mental note that they were open from eight until one, then from five until seven. Which pretty much made sense: it was too hot in the summer afternoons to do anything other than laze about in the shade, and most shops in this part of the world simply shut.

She bought salad, vegetables, olive oil and balsamic vinegar in the *alimentari*, then queued up at the deli counter to buy cold meat, cheese, fresh pasta, and home-made pesto. She stopped off to buy fresh bread in the bakery, and bought a bagful of the gorgeous-looking pastries for Matt, then took a photograph of the contents of her basket and sent it to her mother and sisters.

Today's lunch and dinner.

She added a second text to Posy.

Am putting your garden in order to say thanks for letting me stay at the villa. Love you! x

Then she headed back up the hill. The last house out of town and at the end of the lane that led directly to Villa Rosa was a white cottage. Hoping that she'd got it right, Immi knocked on the door.

There was a long pause before the door opened to reveal Gloria Stark, propping herself up with a stick.

'Mrs Stark? Good morning. I don't know if you remember me from the wedding,' Immi said.

'Andie's sister—I remember,' Gloria said with a smile. 'Imogen, isn't it?'

She nodded. 'Everyone calls me Immi.'

'Then you must call me Gloria, Immi. Matt said you were coming to stay at the villa.'

'I wanted to call in to say thank you for the bread and the milk yesterday,' Immi said. 'I brought you some flowers, and some pastries for Matt to say thanks for coming to my rescue last night.'

'When you rang the alarm bell?'

'When I tripped over the cord without realising what it was,' Immi said ruefully. 'I thought he was a burglar and I nearly hit him with a saucepan.'

Gloria laughed. 'He told me. Really, he should've left you a note about the bell. Come in and have some coffee. I'll put the machine on.'

'Thank you. Can I do anything to help?' Immi asked as she closed the front door behind her and followed Gloria's slow progress into the kitchen.

'I'm fairly independent nowadays, thanks to Matt,' Gloria said with a smile, 'though even he can't make a system to lift a vase out of a cupboard and arrange flowers for me.'

'I can do that,' Immi said, 'if you tell me which cupboard.'

'Thank you. How do you like your coffee? Latte? Cappuccino? Sugar?'

'Cappuccino, no sugar, please.'

While she was arranging the flowers, Gloria said, 'Gloria, time for coffee. Cappuccino.'

Immi heard the click of a switch and saw a light appear on the side of what looked like a very expensive coffee machine. 'That's a voice-controlled coffee machine?' she asked, surprised.

'Matt's design,' Gloria said.

'And, forgive me for being rude, but did you just call it Gloria?'

Gloria laughed. 'That's actually the name of the system—you need a "wake word" so it recognises your voice and then the command.' She indicated the unassuming little black box on a low shelf. 'Matt named it after me.'

'So you just tell that little box to make coffee, and it switches on the coffee machine for you?'

'You need to tell it which pod to use,' Gloria said. 'But basically that's it.'

'Wow. Cleve said that Matt did something clever with technology, but I wasn't expecting it to be that amazing.'

'The system's brilliant. I can't do everything for myself,' Gloria said, 'but I can do so much more than I could fifteen years ago.'

'Fifteen years?'

'I was diagnosed with rheumatoid arthritis when Matt was twelve,' Gloria explained, 'and by the time he was fifteen I was practically crippled by it.' She grimaced. 'I try to walk around the house with my stick as much as possible, to keep my joints mobile, but if I'm going out I use a wheelchair because it helps me pace myself. If I have to stand for a long time, I struggle.'

'I'm sorry,' Immi said.

'It could be worse,' Gloria said. 'I can manage to do my own shopping in the village, and the only days where I don't do physio is during a bad flare-up, when the inflammation makes my joints too swollen and painful. Most of the time, the medication keeps it under reasonable control, but I still get flare-ups. The climate here suits me really well and, thanks to Matt's inventions, I can do a lot more things for myself than I used to. Not being able to turn a light on or off, or change the thermostat when I was too hot or too cold, or even walk across the room and close my own curtains...' She shook her head, grimacing. 'Well, it made me feel so useless and frustrated. Having as much equipment as possible controlled by voice has given me a lot of my independence back.'

'And Matt designed the system by himself?'

'He's a clever lad,' Gloria said.

'And he's a nice guy,' Immi said. 'Andie said he saved her from sticking her head into a cupboard full of spider webs. And my twin's the walking definition of an arachnophobe.'

Gloria smiled. 'Which sounds as if you're not?'

'I,' Immi said, 'am a rescuer of spiders. And I'm still trying to convince her of how beautiful spider webs are in autumn, first thing in the morning when they're all glittering with dew.'

Gloria smiled. 'Your cappuccino's ready. Do you want to give the voice control stuff a try and make one for me?'

'I'd love to. What do I do?'

'Put a mug in the middle there,' Gloria directed. 'I'll have the same as you, but with one sugar, please.'

'OK.' Immi carefully removed the mug, replaced it with a fresh one and said, 'Gloria, time for coffee. Cappuccino, one sugar.'

The machine duly made the coffee as requested.

'That's mind-blowing,' Immi said.

'I probably take it for granted, but you're right. It's amazing to be able to get a cup of coffee without having to struggle with taps, a kettle or the lid of a jar, especially if I'm having a flare-up in my hands.' Gloria smiled at her. 'Let's have coffee in the living room.'

Immi took the mugs and followed her. 'Does Matt sell those coffee machines commercially? My dad would love something like this.' She smiled. 'Dad's a bit of a gadget fiend.'

'Then he's right in the middle of Matt's target market,' Gloria said. 'Though I should warn you, this stuff isn't cheap.' She paused. 'Unless you're disabled. Matt's set up a charity specifically to fund and install systems for people in my position.'

'That's a really nice thing to do,' Immi said. The more she was discovering about Matt Stark, the nicer she thought he was. The complete opposite to Stephen. A decent, caring human being who tried to make the world a better place.

'There's a little black box in each room—it's basically a network—so I can say the commands anywhere in the house, and I can set up any new instructions using an app on my phone. The whole thing works with a computer network and a cloud,' Gloria said. 'I'll show you.'

Immi was amazed to discover that the lights, the curtains, the air conditioning and the heating and the door opening were all controlled by voice. 'I've seen people using a more limited version of voice control on a phone, mainly for dictating emails, but I wouldn't know where to begin developing something like this.'

'He started with the lights and added things bit by bit. He was always good with science,' Gloria said. 'And even as a toddler he was obsessed with the moon and the stars. I always thought he'd end up doing something at NASA or the European Space Agency. He had a place at Cambridge to read astrophysics.'

That, Imogen thought, explained the stargazing.

'But he turned it down,' Gloria said with a sigh. 'He wouldn't leave me and the girls.'

Immi remembered Matt mentioning his four younger sisters at the wedding. So if he was the oldest and he'd been only fifteen when Gloria's illness grew so severe as to cripple her, his sisters would still have been quite young. Where, she wondered, was his father while all this was happening? Though it felt way too intrusive to ask. It was none of her business.

'Matt's been my carer since he was fifteen,' Gloria said. 'And, thanks to him, I'm settled here in Baia di Rose.' She smiled ruefully, 'Though he worries too much about me. I'm doing fine.'

'You're doing fine, Mum, because I'm here to keep an eye on you,' a deep voice pointed out, and Matt strode into the room. 'Good morning, Immi.'

Today he was wearing faded jeans and a white shirt with the sleeves rolled halfway up his arms. He looked approachable. *Touchable.*

And she needed to get a grip.

The almost-kiss at the wedding had been an aberration on both sides. And if Matt was his mother's full-time carer as well as being an inventor, he had no room in his life for any kind of relationship.

Immi didn't want to get involved with anyone right now, either. Not until she knew what she wanted to do with her life.

Then she realised that he was waiting for her to answer him, and she was probably wearing the expression of a stunned fish. 'Good morning, Matt. I brought you some pastries to thank you for rescuing me yesterday. They're in the kitchen.'

'And she brought me flowers,' Gloria chipped in.

'That was kind of you,' he said.

But his eyes were unreadable. Did he think she'd been prying?

'It's the least I can do,' she said, feeling awkward and as if she was intruding on his privacy.

'I've just been showing Immi how your system works. Will you join us for coffee?' Gloria asked.

'Of course.' He went into the kitchen, and came back bearing a mug of coffee for himself and with the *cornetti* on a plate. Immi noticed that he made sure that his mother was comfortable and her coffee and pastries were in easy reach.

'So are you staying at the villa long, Immi?' Gloria asked.

'I'm not sure,' Immi said. 'I just needed a bit of time to myself right now, and Sofia's garden— well, Posy's garden, now,' she corrected herself, 'needs sorting out, so it makes sense for me to do that at the same time.'

Gloria didn't push to ask why Immi needed time to herself; either Matt had already told her and she was being tactful, or she was kind enough to guess that it was something Immi really didn't want to talk about.

'The villa's a bit of a shadow of its former self, I believe,' Gloria said. 'Is Posy planning to renovate it and live there?'

'I don't know,' Immi said. 'A lot of the upstairs rooms are shrouded in dustsheets so I haven't really bothered going up there, and the downstairs needs a lot of work. I know my other sisters had a hand in fixing some of the plastering and glazing and what have you while they were staying, so I guess I ought to do something as well.'

'Matt's good at painting,' Gloria said. 'And woodwork. He made the decking around Sofia's hot spring, so it was easier for her to access it—and for me, as she kindly let us use it as well. You wouldn't mind giving Immi a hand with some painting, would you, Matt?'

Oh, help. Now his mother had asked him straight out, he could hardly say no. But having Matt around at the villa would be bad for her peace of mind, Immi thought—because then she'd keep thinking about that almost-kiss at the wedding. Wondering what it would be like if it happened again, now that she was free...

Hopefully he'd make some excuse that he was too busy to do anything at the villa.

But, to her surprise, he said, 'I could undercoat the bare plasterwork in magnolia.'

'I...er...' Immi said. 'I can't really make decisions about the house on Posy's behalf. It'd be better to ask her.'

But Gloria didn't seem to take any notice of Immi's hesitation. 'All bare plaster needs an undercoat, and magnolia's a good base. Posy can choose whatever she wants for the top coat. That's settled, then,' she said with a smile.

Thankfully Gloria then started talking about the village and its history. Immi did her best to pay attention, but she found herself sneaking little glances at Matt.

He really was beautiful, with those soulful dark eyes and a mouth that practically promised pleasure. Added to a quick mind and a kind, caring, genuine personality, it made him irresistible.

Except neither of them was really in a place to start any kind of relationship. Maybe if they'd met at another time, in another place, it might've been different. But all they could really be to each other was a temporary neighbour. Maybe a friend.

When she'd finished her coffee, Immi excused herself. 'I really shouldn't take up your whole morning.'

'And you said you were busy with the garden,' Gloria said. 'I'm taking up your time.'

'It was a pleasure,' Immi said, meaning it.

'Call in any time,' Gloria said.

Matt made polite noises, but Immi noticed that he didn't actually repeat his mother's offer. Maybe he, too, thought it would be safer to keep some distance between them.

'Lovely to see you,' Immi said brightly, and let Gloria see her to the door.

Back at the villa, she tossed some courgettes,

aubergines and peppers in a mixture of balsamic vinegar and oil, and roasted them in the ancient oven while she worked out her plan for cutting back the shrubs and changed back into her scruffy gardening clothes. She left the vegetables cooling in a covered dish, then hunted in the garage for a small saw so she could make a start on the shrubs.

Cutting the branches back with a mixture of secateurs and the saw kept her so busy that she completely lost track of time. It was only when she emptied the wheelbarrow that she realised that she was hot, probably should've reapplied her sunscreen ages ago, and was really thirsty. And her stomach had just started to rumble. She wasn't wearing a watch, so she had no idea what the time was; not that it mattered what time she took a lunch break, because she only had herself to please. But when she walked into the house, she smelled fresh paint rather than the scent of roasted vegetables. Plus there was classical music

coming from the drawing room—and she definitely hadn't left any music on.

Frowning, she walked into the drawing room
to see Matt there, wearing a pair of shorts and
nothing else, and wielding a paintbrush.

The muscles of his back were beautiful, and
her mouth went dry.

Although she hadn't spoken, maybe something
else had made him aware that he was no longer
alone, and he turned round to face her.

Her mouth went drier still. Matt had a wash-
board abdomen and a definite six-pack, and a
light sprinkling of hair on his chest. And his bare
feet were beautiful, too. Desire zinged through
her.

'I…er…'

Oh, help.

She really hoped that what she was thinking
wasn't written all over her face. And that he
couldn't read minds.

'I made a start on the painting,' he said.

She'd noticed. And how.

He could've graced just about any magazine ad. Women would fall in droves at his feet.

And, oh, for pity's sake, what was she doing, ogling him like this? Though she could practically hear Portia's voice in her head: *There's nothing wrong with appreciating a fine male form.*

'Uh-huh,' was all she could manage.

'You look as if you've had a successful time in the garden.' He walked over to her and brushed something from her face, then gave her a rueful smile. 'Sorry—I meant to get rid of a smudge of dirt for you, but I've just made it worse. I forgot about the paint.'

That brief touch had made her skin tingle, and flustered her so much that it was a while before she realised he was waiting for her to speak.

'Oh—I guess I'd better find some turps.'

'It's emulsion. It'll wash off with soap and water,' he reassured her.

'Back in a tick,' she said, glad of the excuse to flee. And she was even gladder to feel the cool water against her heated skin. It helped to get her common sense back.

The mirror wasn't reassuring. Her hair was all over the place, there were a couple of red patches on her skin where she'd just started to burn, and her face was red and sweaty.

A million miles away from how she normally was in the office, cool and calm in a power suit.

But maybe it was a good thing that she looked a mess. It might make Matt forget about that near-kiss, the night of Andie and Cleve's wedding.

On the other hand, he was painting her sister's house out of sheer kindness. She could hardly sit there and eat her lunch while he was working. It'd be worse than rude—it'd be selfish and mean, which wasn't her at all.

She dried her face and hands and went back to the drawing room. 'I was just going to have a break for lunch. It's only salad and bread, but would you like to join me?'

'Thank you. That'd be nice.'

'Help yourself to anything you need in the

bathroom. It'll take me five minutes to get everything together,' she said.

While he went to wash the paint from his own skin, she picked some basil from the enormous bush growing in what had clearly once been a much-loved herb garden, tore the leaves roughly and tossed them with the roasted vegetables, then crumbled some ricotta over them and mixed the lot together. She put the bowl on the large kitchen table and put fresh bread on a wooden board next to.it. By the time Matt came back into the kitchen, she'd laid the table, filled two glasses with water and composed herself completely.

And to her relief he'd pulled on an old T-shirt. It was going to be a lot easier having a conversation with him when she wasn't being distracted by that gorgeous musculature.

'It's nothing fancy,' she warned. Though it had taken her a lot of work to reach the point where she could enjoy food again, from simple sourdough bread through to more elaborate meals. 'Um—I didn't bother buying any wine, but I'm

sure I can root around to see if Sofia left anything in the cellar.'

'Water's fine,' he said. 'And that looks lovely.'

'Help yourself.' She gestured to the chair opposite hers, and waited for him to load his own
plate before adding salad to hers and taking a
photograph on her phone.

'Something for social media?' he asked.

'Something like that,' she said. It was easier to
let him believe that she was a pretentious foodie
than to admit the truth: that she'd had an eating
disorder in her teens, and needed the picture to
stop her mother and sisters worrying that the
stress of the last few weeks would push her back
into a bad place again. 'It's kind of you to do the
painting. I really wasn't expecting that.'

'I'm at a bit of a loose end at the moment,' he
said.

'But aren't you busy with all your voice-control systems?' she asked.

'The business practically runs itself,' he said.
'I have good staff. And I'm at the stage now

where developing anything new would really be for the sake of development rather than being of real practical use.' He shrugged. 'Unless I go to the next step. I'm not sure I really want to work with robotics—or that the world's quite ready for putting an implant under their skin.'

She blinked. 'Implants?'

'Microchips, really, just put under the skin,' he explained.

'Like you do with dogs?'

'Pretty much,' he agreed. 'Except it'd have a greater scope of information. So, say, if you wanted to go through an airport gate, you'd wave the hand with the microchip over the sensor, which would give your ID to the airline's computer system. The system could check that you were booked in and then open the gate for you.'

'That sounds a wee bit Big Brother-ish,' she said.

'It's probably Orwell's worst nightmare,' he agreed. 'I was thinking of more practical uses at home rather than commercial stuff. But at the

moment it feels like reinventing the wheel, because my system can already do the sort of thing
that the microchip would do. And both systems
need the internet in order to work.' He shrugged.
'Maybe I need to look at different forms of de-
livery.'

But it didn't sound as if his heart was in it.
'You're bored,' she said.

'At a crossroads,' he corrected. 'Looking at
my options.'

Which was exactly what she was doing.

Then she made the mistake of looking him in
the eye.

Awareness of him zinged through every pore,
and her skin felt too tight.

This was crazy. She barely knew the man.
They hadn't even met half a dozen times yet.
But at the same time it felt as if she'd known
him for ever.

'Options are good,' she said, aware that her
voice was croaky. 'And lists. Pros and cons.'

'Critical path analysis,' he said. 'So you know

what has to be done before you can take each step and don't end up with a gap or a missed deadline.'

'Absolutely,' she agreed. Business talk. This was something she knew well and was comfortable with. So why did it feel as if they were talking about something much more personal?

'So how's the garden coming along?' he asked.

'It's going to take time. But I like a challenge.'

And then she wished she'd put it another way when his expression seemed to heat at the word 'challenge'.

She needed to cool this down again. Fast. 'It's kind of you to help with the painting.'

He shrugged. 'It needs doing and I haven't got a lot of demands on my time right now.' He paused. 'So did you and your sisters come here a lot when you were younger?'

She nodded. 'Most summers. Sofia was great. Even though she was godmother only to Posy, she treated the four of us all the same. She let us play dress-up with all her gorgeous clothes—she knew we'd be careful with them—and we spent our days here swimming, sunbathing, running around the garden and the beach, and sitting in the hot spring. There was never any pressure here.' Which was why she, Portia and Andie had all instinctively gravitated here when their lives had suddenly gone skewed: to a place where they had nothing but happy memories.

'A time when life was simpler,' he said. 'That's a good thing to recapture.'

'You can't go back,' Immi said. 'But I think you can learn from the past.'

'Maybe,' he said. And there was deep, deep sadness in his eyes.

She gestured to the salad bowl. 'Help yourself to more.'

'No, I'm fine. I'd better get on with the painting. Thanks for lunch.'

What had she said to make him suddenly back off like this?

But it felt too awkward to ask.

'I'll give you a hand clearing up,' he said.

'No need. I'll just put the salad in the fridge. I'll sort out the rest later tonight.'

He smiled, then. 'I had you pegged as a neat freak. Someone who'd never leave an empty mug unwashed.'

Ouch. That sounded exactly like how she was back in England. She lived her whole life by rules. 'Different place, different rules,' she said lightly. 'I'll catch you later.'

She stacked the dirty crockery, glasses and cutlery by the sink, covered the salad bowl and put it in the fridge, then headed back out to the garden. She remembered just in time to reapply her sunscreen, then lost herself in her work, cutting back the overgrown branches and freeing some of the ivy that threatened to choke the plants.

When she got back to the villa, Matt was gone. So was the pile of dirty dishes: he'd washed up and stacked all the clean stuff on the table. And there was a note by the kettle.

Will be watching the sunset tonight, if you want to join me on the bench.

Adrenalin prickled down her spine.

Was he just being polite? Or was it his way of saying that he knew things were complicated for both of them, but he'd like to spend time with her and was leaving the decision up to her?

Or maybe she was just overthinking things.

Maybe the sheer romance of this place was getting to her—L'Isola dei Fiori, the island of flowers. Wasn't there some kind of crazy romantic legend about the rock arch on the beach?

She was still no closer to a decision by the time she'd finished the salad in the fridge and soaked her tired muscles in the ancient bath. But then, instead of getting into her pyjamas, she found herself putting on a simple summery skirt and top.

Face value, she reminded herself. This was just watching the sunset in the company of someone else whose life was at a crossroads. An acquaintance, possibly a friend.

And then she headed out to the quiet little arbour in the garden.

CHAPTER FOUR

MATT STARED OUT to sea, wondering if Immi would come and watch the sunset with him or whether she'd stay away. It had been sheer impulse that had led him to write that note. Probably a crazy one. And an even crazier one that had made him bring a bottle of rosé wine and two glasses with him.

But then he looked up and she was there.

'Hi.' She gave him a shy smile.

'Hi.' He moved up on the bench to make room for her.

'Thanks for asking me to come and watch the sunset with you,' she said. 'We're so far from the sea in Cambridge. I don't get to see this kind of thing that often.'

'It's one of the perks of living on a small island.

You're never that far from the sea.' He offered her one of the glasses. 'I wasn't sure if you preferred red or white, but it's summer so I brought rosé.'

'Rosé's good, thanks.' She smiled. 'I had my first sip of rosé wine here at the villa. Andie and I must've been all of ten, Posy was nine and Portia was twelve. Sofia made us spritzers—they were probably ninety-five per cent lemonade, but the four of us all thought we were so grown up and sophisticated. She made us posh canapés and we all dressed up and had a party on her terrace, just the five of us, with citronella candles burning. We loved it.'

'My sisters would've loved that, too,' he said, smiling back, and filled her glass before doing the same with his own. 'Well. To us, to crossroads, and to choosing the right way to go next.' He lifted his glass.

'To us, to crossroads, and to choosing the right way to go next,' she echoed, chinking her glass lightly against his. She took a sip. 'This is good.'

'It's from a vineyard just over on the mainland,' he said. 'How's the gardening going? I noticed your pile of branches is getting quite a lot bigger.'

'I was going to ask you about that,' she said. 'Are there any local laws about when I can have a bonfire?'

'No, but obviously the wind has to be in the right direction—and up here it can switch very quickly.' He paused. 'I can ask around and see if anyone has a garden shredder you could borrow. That'd be a safer option.'

'And better for the garden, because I can use the chippings as mulch. Thanks. I'd appreciate that.'

'So is the gardening helping?' He cringed even as he said it. His mother always said he talked too much. And that had been a seriously intrusive question.

'It's been good to have something else to focus on. I've made one firm decision today—I'm going to put my flat on the market when I go back to England. I want to live somewhere with a proper garden, not just a window box.' She smiled ruefully. 'I guess it's one step away from the crossroads.'

'One step's a start.'

She lapsed into silence, and he sighed inwardly. The awkwardness was all his fault. 'Sorry. I didn't mean to pry.'

'You weren't prying.' She took another sip of wine. 'And maybe you're right. Maybe talking to someone who isn't part of the whole mess will help me untangle it a bit. If the offer's still there.'

'Of course it is.'

'Thanks.' She paused. 'But I don't want to be a victim, so no pitying me under *any* circumstances, right?'

'Right,' he agreed.

'At Andie's wedding... I kind of knew something wasn't right, but I told myself I was just being paranoid and letting the stress of organising my own wedding get to me,' Immi said. 'But my twin's wedding was utterly perfect: small and private, and I saw that Cleve looked at Andie as if she was the only person in the world.'

Matt had noticed that, too. And he'd been envious. Not in a bad way—he liked Andie enormously, but wasn't in love with her—but in a wistful kind of 'what's it like to really love someone and have them love you all the way back?' way. His own dates had tended to change their mind fairly quickly as soon as they realised that he came as a package. And he was non-negotiable on the package deal.

'I take it your fiancé didn't look at you like that?' he asked.

'Not even close.' She bit her lip. 'And I have to be fair about this, I didn't look at him the way that Andie looks at Cleve, either, so I can't put all the blame on him.'

'And that's why you cancelled the wedding?'

'That wasn't quite enough of a reason.' She paused. 'Stephen let me down.'

He waited, knowing there was more to come.

'Remember, you promised—no pity,' she warned.

'No pity,' he said, careful to keep his voice neutral.

'A few months ago, I overheard his best friend, Jamie, telling him to keep his nose clean, until I'd said "I do" and he'd got the corner office.' She blew out a breath. 'I tried to tell myself that Jamie was making some kind of weird blokey joke I didn't understand, and I was seeing shadows where there weren't any. But then Stephen didn't come to Andie's wedding. And it made me think: if someone's quite ambitious and he's engaged to the boss's daughter, surely he's going to be there at her twin's wedding instead of using work as an excuse to avoid it?'

Exactly what Matt had thought. He'd wondered about the absent fiancé, and why he was putting business before the woman he was about to marry. 'It's a fair point,' Matt said, trying hard not to sound judgemental.

'I thought maybe he was getting cold feet about

the wedding. I mean, I was getting jittery about it, too. It seemed to snowball and take over everything, and we never seemed to talk about anything any more except the wedding. So I thought I'd come home early from a business trip to surprise him. The plan was, we'd have a romantic dinner out and spend some time together without even mentioning the W-word.' Her face was tight. 'I guess the surprise was mainly mine.'

'He wasn't at home?'

'Oh, he was there, all right.' Her voice was very, very quiet. 'And there was a trail of another woman's clothes through my flat.'

'Hang on. He cheated on you in your own flat?' Matt was truly shocked.

'Uh-huh. And it turned out it wasn't the first time.' She looked away. 'Which was obviously what Jamie meant about keeping his nose clean.'

Matt wanted to punch the guy. Very, very hard. Except violence didn't solve anything. It didn't miraculously turn the other person into someone decent, and it made you feel as if you'd sunk to their level when you found out you'd broken their nose. He'd learned that one the hard way.

'No pity,' she reminded him.

'I'm not pitying you,' he promised. 'Though I'm angry on your behalf.'

'Join the queue,' she said wryly. 'Portia wanted to scalp him, and Dad wanted to punch him.'

'Violence doesn't solve anything.'

'It wouldn't make him change the way he behaved. And it wouldn't make me trust him again.'

'It sounds to me as if you had a lucky escape,' he said. 'He would've made you miserable.'

'True.' She paused. 'He said I wasn't enough for him.'

Her voice was even and her tone was measured, but he'd seen that flicker of sadness in her eyes. The hurt that she'd been found wanting.

Which was crazy. Imogen Marlowe would definitely be enough for any man. Not that there was any way for him to tell her that. You didn't hit on a woman who'd only recently discovered she'd been cheated on by the man she was going to marry and had a broken heart. 'That sounds like an excuse. Self-justification from someone who knew he was in the wrong, and decided that attack is the best form of defence. More like, he was a selfish, lying scumbag who didn't deserve you,' Matt said.

'Thank you. Though I wasn't fishing for compliments.'

'It wasn't meant to be one. Some people,' he said, thinking of his father, 'aren't capable of thinking about anyone else's needs. They come first, second, last—and everywhere in between.'

'That sounds personal.'

'Yeah.' And he didn't want to talk about that. He didn't want to be put on a pedestal as the guy who'd given up his dreams at the age of fifteen and stepped in to support his family. Because any decent person would've done the same thing, in his shoes. What else was he meant to have done—let his sisters go into care and left his disabled mother to fend for herself? Plus he hadn't exactly been squeaky clean. His father could have taken him to court for actual bodily harm, after Matt had punched him and broken his nose.

He switched the focus back to her. 'You did the right thing, calling off the wedding. Though it can't have been much fun for you, having to cancel everything.'

'At least cancelling it all myself meant I knew it had been done,' she said.

'Your ex didn't do anything to help?'

'It was my choice to cancel the wedding.'

'As a consequence of his behaviour.' Matt blew out a breath. 'He sounds a real charmer.'

'Oh, he can be. He spent a week trying to charm me out of it. Fresh flowers on my desk every morning—though he never actually sent my favourite flowers,' she said. 'I gave them to the local nursing homes to brighten up someone else's day.'

Matt was still trying to work out how you could be about to marry someone and still not have a clue what her favourite flowers were. Was the man completely unobservant? 'That was kind.'

'Not really—I didn't want them, but putting them in the bin felt wrong. At least that way other people got the pleasure of the flowers,' she said.

'What happened when he realised the charm wasn't working?'

'The flowers stopped. Then there was a week of sniping.' She grimaced. 'Then Mum and Dad came back from India, and I had a week of trying to keep the peace.

'This was the week I was supposed to get married,' Immi said. 'And I guess part of me feels as if I'm running away from it all.'

'Or maybe you're putting some sensible distance between yourself and a really unpleasant situation,' he said.

'I'd booked this week off anyway, and the next three weeks,' Immi said. 'I really didn't want to be in Cambridge, with everyone pitying me and tiptoeing round me and asking me how I was.

Posy offered me a bolt hole here at the villa.' She gave him a rueful smile. 'And working in a garden's the best stress-reliever I know.'

'A month in the sun, doing something you love,' he said. 'That sounds sensible.'

'Self-indulgent, too,' she said wryly. 'But hopefully in that month I can work out what to do now with my career.'

What did her career have to do with her broken engagement? He didn't understand. 'Andie said you worked for your family business.'

'Marlowe Aviation,' she confirmed.

'So you're thinking of a total change because you're not happy there?' he guessed.

'I love planes more than anything else in the world,' she said, 'and I love working at my family business.'

'So why are you thinking about a change in career?'

'Because,' she said quietly, 'Stephen was my father's temporary number two while he and Mum were away in India.'

Matt hadn't realised that her ex-fiancé had worked with her, too. He frowned. 'But surely he's done the decent thing and resigned, then found himself another job somewhere else?'

'There aren't that many light aircraft manu-facturers in England, so opportunities like being Dad's second-in-command are pretty thin on the ground,' Immi explained. 'So, no, he hasn't re-signed. Why would he give up his dream job?'

Because he'd behaved incredibly badly and hurt Immi. Any decent person would leave, in those circumstances. But then, any decent person wouldn't have cheated on her in the first place. Matt thought about it. 'I'm guessing your father can't just ask him to leave the company.'

'No, because what he did was nothing to do with work. If Dad sacked him, Stephen would be able to sue us for constructive dismissal.' She sighed. 'Which means I'm going to have to be the one to leave.'

Which clearly she didn't want to do; and hadn't

she said that opportunities in aviation weren't that common?

'I only ever really wanted to work at Marlowe Aviation, when I was growing up,' she said wistfully. 'Posy was always wrapped up in her dancing and Portia loved the bright lights—actually, I thought she'd be a children's author because she used to tell us stories all the time about our soft toys when we were little. But Andie and I were plane-mad right from the start. You know how kids make cars or houses out of big boxes? Andie and I made planes instead, and we had little flying helmets and goggles and bomber jackets for our teddies. Who, of course, were also twins and ace pilots.'

Matt could just imagine it, and smiled. 'Cleve said he remembered the first time he ever met Andie, when she'd just landed a plane. So you're a pilot, too, like her?'

'Not in quite the same way. Marlowe Aviation manufactures light aircraft, the sort that firms like Cleve's use for short-haul flights and light cargo,' she explained. 'We make planes for flying schools, and companies who do photographic and survey work. Originally Andie was training to be an aircraft designer and she was going to launch a new range for us—a design that could be tweaked so the plane could be used for cargo or as an air ambulance. But then she went to work for Cleve. I studied business management and organisation, so that's what I do.' She smiled. 'But, yes, I've got my pilot's licence. I was a bit later than Andie because I...' She flapped a dismissive hand. 'Well, I messed up my A levels and had to resit them.'

'It happens to a lot of people,' he said.

'I guess. Anyway, it means I can do the test flights for any plane we build.'

'Hang on. So you're a test pilot?' He blinked. 'That's impressive.'

'Only some of the time, and it's not that impressive. I'm just taking the plane through a set of manoeuvres and seeing how it performs, to spot if there are any tweaks we need to make.

Though I admit it's my favourite bit of my job,'
she said. 'There's something about flying. Just
you and a small plane and the air. It's quiet and
peaceful and lovely, and you can see the whole
world spreading out before you.'

He could see the passion in her face. She
seemed to light up when she was talking about
flying. And all of a sudden he found himself
wondering how he could put that expression in
her eyes.

Oh, for pity's sake. He wasn't in a position
to start any kind of relationship. In less than a
month, she'd be going back to England and he
might never see her again. Even if he did work
out how he could follow his dreams without hurting anyone—well, the last thing he needed was a
commitment that meant he'd have to put everything on hold again.

He and Immi were destined to live parallel
lives.

All he could offer her was friendship. And

maybe bounce some ideas with her to help her decide what she wanted to do next with her life.

'Could you go and be a pilot for someone else?'

'Like Andie did with Cleve?' She wrinkled her nose. 'Probably but, as I said, there aren't that many opportunities—and I like working in my family business.'

And it wasn't just the family history, the idea of being the third generation to manufacture planes; Immi genuinely liked her colleagues and the atmosphere at Marlowe Aviation.

Though, if she was totally honest with herself, working at the family business was also a kind of safety net. Somewhere she felt supported, where she knew people were looking out for her and she had less chance of slipping back into her old bad ways if life threw her a curveball. She'd needed every bit of that support, these last few weeks. There had been days when she'd had to force herself to swallow a few mouthfuls—and she'd made herself do it because she knew what came next if she didn't. No way was she letting Stephen push her back that far.

'It doesn't seem fair that you should have to leave your own family business because of your ex,' Matt said.

'It's that or having to put up with him every single day, and trying to keep the peace between him and Dad. Last week was more than enough for me. Priya—our HR manager—is brilliant with Dad, and he probably listens more to her because she's not his daughter,' Immi admitted wryly. 'She says things are calming down a bit. But I'm pretty sure that, as soon as I go back, the whole thing's going to blow up again.' She gave him a rueful smile. 'So that doesn't leave me much choice. I need to find something else to do. Maybe working with vintage aircraft at one of the museums—but again, it's a world where there aren't many openings and most of them are for voluntary work. I want to be able to support myself.' She sighed. 'So maybe I'll have to retrain and do something else entirely.'

'What would you do? From what I've seen of the garden, you know what you're doing there.'

'I'm strictly amateur,' she said. 'I love gardening, but it's always been what I do to get rid of stress.' Ever since rehab, where one of the therapists had suggested that she tried her hand at gardening, and Immi had discovered that she loved being able to make things grow and blossom almost as much as she loved flying. 'I'd need qualifications before I could get a proper job in horticulture.'

'And I'm guessing you'd rather work with planes?'

She nodded. 'It's always been my big love.'

'There's no chance that your ex will do the decent thing and leave?' Matt asked.

'I doubt it,' Immi said with a sigh. 'He's pretty much been thwarted in his ambitions to take over Marlowe's from Dad, so I guess staying in the firm as a thorn in everyone's side is his way of paying us back. And we can't do a thing about it unless he does something that's against his terms of contract.'

'Or you could restructure the firm, maybe, and make him redundant?'

'And then we have to prove that his job no longer exists. Which would be a tricky line to walk, right now. Unless we made other people redundant, which isn't really on the cards, he could claim we'd targeted him and it was constructive dismissal.' She grimaced. 'Short of hiring a hit-man—and, believe me, there have been days when I've wished I could—we're stuck with him until he decides to leave.'

'Let's hope he develops a conscience.'

'I wouldn't put any money on that if I were you,' Immi said dryly. 'There's more chance of a freak lightning strike—and how bad is it that I've actually hoped for that?'

'Considering how he let you down, probably not that bad in the scheme of things,' Matt said, and refilled her glass.

'Thank you. For both,' she said, and took a

sip of wine. 'And now can we please change the subject?'

'Sure. And if I think of any bright ideas about your career, I'll let you know.'

'Thanks.'

'I was going to ask you a favour,' he said. 'Mum's had a couple of flare-ups this week, and in the past she's found that a soak in the hot springs helps a bit with the inflammation. Is it OK if she uses Sofia's pool?'

'Of course it is.' She smiled at him. 'How ridiculous is it that I forgot about the pool? I guess I was concentrating more on the garden and didn't think about heading down to the beach.' She paused. 'But I remember the path down there being a bit—well, rocky. Isn't that going to be a bit tough for your mum?'

'I did some work on the path and installed decking,' he said. 'It made the place more stable for Sofia—who, of course, would never admit to feeling in the slightest bit old or frail, but I'm used to spotting the signs with my mum. Sofia used to come and spend time at our place, chatting to my mum, so I got Mum to persuade her to let me help. In Sofia's mind, she was being kind and making the changes so she could help a neighbour; but it also kept her safe so Mum wasn't worrying about it.'

'You're one of life's nice guys, aren't you?' Immi asked. 'And I mean that in a good way, not a snarky way.'

'I'm not always nice,' Matt said.

Immi didn't believe that for a second. But what she didn't understand was why Matt hadn't been snapped up at a very young age. He ticked every single box: clever, kind, handsome, honourable... So had someone broken his heart?

She could hardly ask straight out.

Anyway, it was none of her business. Plus she knew he was at a crossroads: the last thing he needed was a rebound crush from someone old enough to know better. 'You wouldn't be human if you were,' she said lightly. 'We all have our dark side.'

'Yeah.'

They lapsed into a relatively companionable silence, watching the sky turn all shades of orange and red and then fade to peach and rose as the sun set.

He nodded over at the horizon. 'The show's pretty much over. I'll walk you back to the house.'

Even though Immi was pretty sure she knew the way back now and could avoid the area where the wall had crumbled, she appreciated the company. 'Thanks.' She followed him back through the narrow path to the villa.

'I'll bring Mum over to the pool tomorrow at about eleven, then, if that's OK?' Matt asked.

'That's fine. And you're both very welcome to stay for lunch,' she said.

He frowned. 'We can't impose on you like that.'

'No imposition. You saved me from painting walls and messing up all over the floor,' she said. 'And your mum made me coffee this morning. It's my turn to do the hospitality.'

'She'll love that. Thank you,' he said. 'I'll see you tomorrow.'

For a moment, she thought he was going to dip his head and kiss her on the cheek. And it shocked her how much she wanted him to do that. How much she wanted to feel his mouth against her skin, his arms wrapped round her.

But then he took a step back. *'Buona sera. Goodnight,'* he said.

'Buona sera.' And, Immi thought, she was just going to have to ignore the pull she felt towards him. This wasn't going to happen.

CHAPTER FIVE

ON WEDNESDAY MORNING, Immi went into the village early to buy fresh bread and the ingredients for lunch. Back at the villa, she made a chicken cacciatore on Sofia's ancient cooker, and put it in a covered dish to cool and let the flavours infuse during the morning. Then she changed into her scruffy gardening clothes, checked her work plan, jammed on a sun hat and went out to tackle the next set of shrubs.

At eleven, Matt came through the garden with Gloria in her wheelchair.

'Good morning, Immi. Are you joining us in the pool?' Gloria asked.

Immi glanced up at Matt to check that he wouldn't mind her muscling in, and he gave her the tiniest nod.

'I'd love to. I'll just wash the mud off and get changed,' she said, taking off her gardening gloves and laying them down next to her secateurs. 'I'll see you down there.'

Even though her swimsuit was perfectly demure, she borrowed one of Sofia's sarongs to wrap round herself, sliced a lemon into a jug of water and added some ice cubes from the old-fashioned metal tray in the top compartment of the equally old-fashioned fridge, then put the jug on a tray with some glasses and headed down the cliff path to the beach.

Matt and his mother were both already sitting in the rock pool, and Gloria's wheelchair was parked on the decking.

'It's been a while since I was out here,' Immi said. 'I'd forgotten how lovely the cove was.' And how private, with the jetty Ludano had used when he visited Sofia almost hidden away from view.

'I brought us some cold drinks,' she said, and poured them all a glass of water.

'How wonderful. Thank you,' Gloria said.

When she handed a glass to Matt, her fingers accidentally brushed against his, and awareness prickled down her spine. Oh, for pity's sake. Anyone would think she was a teenager, reacting to him in this way. She had to remember that he was simply Sofia's very nice, very kind neighbour. Her friend, perhaps. She wasn't going to be all ridiculous and let herself get smitten by him. He deserved to be a lot more than Rebound Man, and she was going to be *sensible* about this.

Then again, she'd thought she was making a sensible choice when she'd accepted Stephen's proposal. Maybe sensible was overrated.

She set her own glass on the decking and climbed into the rock pool. The water from the hot springs was the perfect temperature to melt away the slight ache in her muscles from all the gardening she'd been doing. 'This is bliss,' she said.

'Isn't it just? It was so nice of Sofia to let us

use the pool,' Gloria said. 'I'm glad your sister doesn't mind.'

'It's the least she can do, given that you've been keeping an eye on the house for her,' Immi said, glad that in this instance she knew exactly what her little sister would say.

Gloria chatted away; Matt was quieter and his face was so expressionless that Immi couldn't tell a thing about his thoughts.

Then Gloria said, 'Now here's me rabbiting on—why don't you two go for a stroll along the beach?'

Matt opened his mouth as if to protest, but Gloria was ready for him. 'I'm absolutely fine sitting here, and you'll be well within shouting distance if I need you.'

Matt gave a helpless shrug. 'We might as well give in, Immi. I've found it's easier to do what she says. Otherwise massive nagging ensues.'

Gloria gave them an unrepentant grin. 'Good choice. Run along, children.' She made shooing motions with her hands.

Immi hauled herself out of the pool; Matt did the same, and together they walked down to the edge of the sea.

Her hand brushed against his, and a tingle of pure desire ran down her arm. She couldn't help glancing at him; his eyes were hidden by his sunglasses, but was that a slash of extra colour in his cheeks? Did he too feel that almost physical pull of attraction?

Though it wasn't a question she could ask right now; and what if she was just deluding herself? Although she was pretty sure Matt would be kind in rejecting her, rejection was something she really couldn't take right now.

Better to keep her distance. To keep herself safe.

'I'd forgotten how private this cove was,' she said. 'I know when Ludano gave Sofia the house, he gave her the right to use the beach as well.'

'Technically,' Matt said, 'this is Crown land, so the beach is open to everyone.'

'But the only real path down here is from the

house, and the land there isn't open to everyone,' she said, 'so practically it's a private beach.' She smiled. 'We loved coming here in the summer when we were kids. We'd make sandcastles, and walk about on the beach looking for the prettiest shells, and look to see if we could find crabs in the rock pools, and run around through the rock arch.' She gestured to the narrow limestone arch that bisected the beach. 'We used to call it Neptune's Arch. Sofia told us he blasted the cliff with his trident to make the arch, and whoever kissed under the arch would find true love.'

Though she really shouldn't have used the K-word—because now she couldn't get it out of her head. The moment when she and Matt had almost kissed, dancing to a slow, soft song at her twin's wedding, when he'd started to dip his head and her lips had parted automatically...

Again, she glanced at him. Was it her imagination, or had his lips just parted?

Imagination, she decided. She was seeing things to distract herself from the chaos of her personal life.

* * *

Whoever kissed under the arch would find true love...

Just a pretty story for the tourists, Matt thought. But now he couldn't get the idea of kissing Immi out of his head—not just that evening when he'd danced with her at the wedding and almost kissed her, but moments since. When he'd brushed that smudge of dirt from her face. When he'd sat with her, looking at the sunset. When she'd told him about the way her ex had betrayed her and he'd wanted to kiss the hurt away.

Every time, he'd told himself it wouldn't be fair to start anything that he couldn't finish. Her life was in England and his was here.

But she was here for another three weeks.

What if, he wondered, he did actually kiss the hurt away? Though suggesting to her that they had a summer fling would sound just a little bit sleazy. And selfish. Which wasn't him.

Better to keep his mouth shut and leave things as they were.

Once they'd walked all round the little cove,

they headed back to the rock pool. Matt helped his mother out of the pool, wrapped a towel round her, and helped her into her wheelchair.

'Come and change in the villa while I finish sorting out lunch,' Immi said.

Matt pushed the wheelchair back up the slope. At the villa, Gloria gratefully accepted Immi's offer to change in Sofia's bedroom, while Matt changed in the bathroom.

Immi boiled the kettle and tipped some couscous in a bowl, then added the hot water and covered it with a plate. She put some tenderstem broccoli on to steam and tipped the chicken cacciatore into a pan to heat through. By the time she'd found cushions to make the hard wooden seating at the kitchen table more comfortable for Gloria and set the table, lunch was ready and so were her guests.

'What can I do?' Matt asked.

'Get the drinks?' Immi suggested. 'There's juice in the fridge, and a bottle of sparkling water.'

Matt sorted out the drinks while Immi served up.

'This is gorgeous, Immi,' Gloria said after her first taste.

'Thanks, but it's one of those dishes that practically looks after itself,' Immi said. 'Which is just as well, because Sofia doesn't seem to have a single mod con in her kitchen. Nothing seems to have changed since the Seventies. I can't quite get used to having to put a kettle on the hot plate instead of switching it on at the mains, and it seems to take ten times as long to boil milk in a pan on the stove than it does in a microwave. It makes me wonder how Sofia managed to cook, when she was frail towards the end.' She frowned. 'I'm guessing she charmed the local shopkeepers into delivering for her— but I also have the feeling she probably lived on sandwiches rather than making herself a meal.'

'Don't forget the gin and the coffee,' Gloria said. 'Sofia made a mean Negroni.'

Matt groaned. 'I can never forget the pair of you singing disco songs from the nineteen-seventies after downing one of those Negronis.'

Gloria spread her hands and grinned. 'How could I not sing a song by my namesake?' She began to hum 'I Will Survive'.

Immi laughed.

'Don't encourage her,' Matt said dolefully.

'Sing away.' Immi took a quick photograph of her plate with her phone.

'Social media?' Gloria asked.

'Absolutely,' Immi fibbed with a smile.

It was nice to have company for lunch; and she knew she was being a coward but it was much easier not to be on her own with Matt. At least then she wouldn't say or do something embarrassing.

'I was very fond of Sofia. She was a genuinely nice woman,' Gloria said. 'Funny, though, I've never really been inside the villa—well, apart from for your sister's wedding. Sofia always used to come to visit me.'

'Would you like to see round the house?' Immi asked.

Gloria smiled. 'I'd love to.'

After lunch, Immi gave them both a guided tour of the ground floor, making sure she took it slowly so Gloria could manage to walk round with the aid of her stick. 'Obviously you've seen Sofia's room and the bathroom.' She took them through to the dining room, where there was a massive table to seat twenty. 'I imagine she had some amazing dinner parties here, but it doesn't feel right to use this enormous table just for me. Anyway, I prefer eating in the kitchen.'

'It's cosier,' Gloria agreed.

Next was the drawing room with its painted fresco. 'This is an amazing room,' she said. 'I love this ceiling; it's just like an evening sky.' She smiled. 'This is what Matt's been working on.'

'The magnolia bits, not the actual painting,' he said dryly.

'And look at all those birds and flowers and tropical trees! It's gorgeous. Someone's clearly fixed the crack in the ceiling, but not touched up the painting.' Gloria looked hopefully at Matt.

'It's way above my pay grade, Mum,' he said gently. 'I just do undercoat and what have you. I'd make a mess of trying to restore the paint on the ceiling. But I agree—this house deserves to be loved again.'

Next, Immi took them through to the hallway. 'This is probably the room in the best condition,' she said. 'Possibly because it's the first one you see and I guess Sofia had her pride.' The room was bright and full of light, with white-painted panelling, bright abstract paintings, a white-tiled floor and the glass-sided staircase curving up to the landing.

'Upstairs is pretty much dust-sheeted everywhere,' Immi said. 'And then there are the attics.'

Matt laughed. 'And their spiders.'

'Wrong twin,' she said, laughing back. 'I happen to like spiders.'

Then she ushered them into the double-height conservatory. There were panes of coloured glass in red, blue, purple, pink, green and yellow dotted here and there, and the sun shone through them to fill the room with colour.

'This is my favourite room in the entire house,' Immi said. 'I love the way the light streams through those coloured panes; it makes it feel as if there's a rainbow of colour in the room. I would have loved to see this in its heyday, filled with plants,' she added wistfully.

'What would you choose, if you had the chance to fill it with plants?' Matt asked.

'That's easy,' she said promptly. 'I'd have a couple of orange trees and ficus for the greenery, climbing stephanotis or jasmine for scent, and plumbago for colour.' She smiled. 'And some giant alliums, because they're so showy and Sofia would have loved them.'

Before opening the double doors to the terrace, she paused, remembering what Matt's mother had said to her about pacing herself while she was walking. 'Gloria, the garden's pretty rambling and it's easy to trip over bits of shrub here and here. Would you prefer to use your chair outside?'

'That's a good idea, love,' Gloria said.

Matt duly fetched the chair and wheeled her out into the garden.

'An easy win to make the place look pretty is the terrace,' Immi said. 'There are loads of terracotta pots in the shed, so I was thinking about going to a garden centre and buying some container plants that don't need much watering. I thought some deep red snapdragons that will bloom all summer long, some lavender for the amazing scent and some silver cinerarias—the foliage will look gorgeous against the pink walls.'

'It sounds as if you're a born gardener,' Gloria said.

'Strictly amateur,' Immi said, 'but I'm not very good at decorating, so this is something I can do to help Posy, whether she decides to keep the house or not. I want to keep it low maintenance so it's not going to cost her a lot of effort or money.'

Gloria indicated the massive pile of branches in the middle of the lawn. 'It looks as if you've been working your way through those shrubs, too.'

'They're all horribly overgrown and need cutting back. So they're not going to look at their best this summer,' Immi said, 'but next summer the garden's going to be gorgeous.'

'I've sourced the garden shredder we talked about,' Matt said. 'I'll bring it round tomorrow and deal with the rubbish for you. Perhaps you could hire it once a week while you're here.'

'That's a good idea—thank you.' She smiled. 'Given that you've both lived here long enough to count as locals, could you recommend a garden centre for my container plants?'

'There's one about five miles down the road to Sant'Angelo,' Gloria said. 'Though that's really too far to walk, especially if you're buying a lot of plants.'

Not wanting Matt's mum to suggest that he should take her, Immi said swiftly, 'There are still some of Sofia's old cars in the garage, and a scooter—Andie said she'd fixed up the two cars a bit, so they're both running.' She grinned. 'I know the scooter works as well, because Portia took it out.'

'Portia,' Matt said, 'is lovely, but she's very slightly scary.'

'She was scarier as a teen, believe you me—the family rebel.' She raised an eyebrow. 'The very first time she took that scooter out, she was way too young to have a licence. She fell off in a ditch, but Alberto—who was one of the couple who used to look after Sofia—was brilliant and covered for her and fixed the dents.'

'So Portia loves motorbikes?' Gloria asked.

'Sort of. Portia sees cars, bikes and planes as modes of transport. So does Posy, really. Andie and I are the ones who'll be poking around the engine and desperate to get behind the wheel to see how it drives or flies,' Immi explained.

Once they were back at the house, Immi made coffee and they sat on the terrace for a bit, enjoying the sea views in the distance.

Finally, Gloria said, 'Thank you for lunch and showing us round. I know you're busy, so we won't keep you from the garden any longer—but you do know you're welcome to pop in any time, don't you?'

'Thank you,' Immi said, meaning it.

She walked to the large four-wheel-drive car with them. Matt helped his mother into the car, then collapsed the wheelchair and put it in the back. 'See you at sunset?' he asked softly.

'I'd like that—and it's my turn to provide the wine tonight. Any preference?' Immi asked.

'Whatever you've got open,' he said. 'See you later.'

She spent the rest of the afternoon working in the garden; but when she'd had a bath and made herself an omelette, she could hear an almost deafening clatter from the conservatory and re-alised that it was pouring with rain.

No chance of watching the sunset together to-night, then.

She wondered if Matt would turn up anyway

to share some wine with her; but he didn't, and Immi was cross with herself for feeling disappointed. It wasn't as if they were dating. Plus he'd already been kind enough with all the painting and sorting out the garden shredder for her. She was just being greedy.

Matt sat in his study and watched the rain. So much for watching the sunset together. The summer storm hadn't been forecast, so he hadn't made any contingency plans with Immi—and, as the landline to Sofia's villa had never been repaired and there was no internet connection or mobile phone signal there, he had no way of getting in touch with her.

Well, apart from possibly Morse code. Would a test pilot need to know Morse code? He had no idea. Plus she'd have to be looking out for the flashes—and what reason would she have to be at the top of the house, looking down the hill towards the village?

He could just turn up anyway.

But that would be making a big assumption.

Tomorrow. He'd see her tomorrow when he took the garden shredder over. And maybe they could talk then.

On Thursday morning, Immi drove the larger of the two cars to the garden centre, hoping that the back would be big enough to fit all the plants and compost she wanted. She chose plants that would look good in pots but wouldn't need lots of dead-heading or watering, bought compost, drove back to the villa and had just about finished sorting out the pots when Matt turned up with the garden shredder.

'Good morning,' he said.

'Good morning,' she replied, feeling slightly wary.

'It's a shame that the rain spoiled the sunset last night.'

Was it her imagination, or did he sound disappointed not to have shared it, too? She took a risk. 'You would've been welcome to come over for a glass of wine anyway.'

Definitely not her imagination, then, because his gorgeous brown eyes darkened slightly. 'I didn't want to make the assumption.'

'Well, now you know.'

His mouth quirked very slightly. 'Indeed.'

And it was suddenly hard to breathe. Not wanting him to guess just how much he affected her, Immi said, 'Do you want a coffee?'

At almost exactly the same time, he asked, 'Where do you want the garden shredder?'

'You, first,' she said, and he repeated his question.

'I didn't know if you had an extension cable reel here, so I brought you one from home.'

'Thank you. The middle of the lawn?' she suggested. 'And would you like a coffee?'

'No, I'm fine,' he said. 'I'll give you a hand with the shredding. It's a bit hard to feed the stuff into the shredder and catch the chips at the same time.'

'Thanks.'

Between them, they got rid of the massive pile of branches, and the chippings were neatly contained in thick plastic sacks. But even though they were both wearing thick gardening gloves, she was aware of every time her hands accidentally brushed against him, or his hands accidentally brushed against her.

'I'll use the chippings as mulch,' she said. 'It'll help keep the weeds at bay.'

Her hand brushed against his as they moved the sacks, and she caught her breath. She glanced up at him, noticing that his eyes were very dark and his mouth was slightly parted; it looked as if he reacted to her in the same way that she reacted to him.

And his voice was slightly husky when he said, 'It's meant to be dry tonight. See you at sunset?'

'Sunset,' she confirmed.

And would tonight be the night when they gave in to the pull and actually kissed? A thrill of sheer anticipation slid down her spine.

'I'd better go. I promised Mum to take her to her book group,' he said. 'See you at sunset.'

When Immi arrived at their bench with a bottle of wine and two glasses, she noticed that he'd brought blankets and cushions. At her raised eyebrow, he said, 'I was planning to stay and watch the stars for a bit after sunset. It's more comfortable lying flat and looking straight up than craning your neck back when sitting on the bench.'

'Uh-huh.' She handed him the glasses and poured the wine. 'To the sunset,' she said softly, and clinked her glass against his.

As usual, they watched the sunset in silence, enjoying the quietness and the view and each other's company.

'Look—the first stars,' she said as the sky darkened.

'Planets,' he corrected with a smile.

'How can you tell the difference?'

'The quick answer is that stars twinkle and planets don't,' he said.

'Seriously?'

'Seriously,' he said. 'It's all to do with our atmosphere interfering with the light coming from the stars. If you saw them from outer space or from a planet without an atmosphere, they wouldn't twinkle. Plus the planets are closer to us than the stars, so they look like discs instead of pinpoints and the atmosphere doesn't interfere with the light source as much.' He paused. 'Stay out here with me for a bit and watch the stars?'

'I'd like that,' she said. 'Though I don't really know the constellations, apart from Orion and the Big Dipper.'

'So you don't navigate by the stars if you fly at night?' he asked.

'In a small plane on my own? No—I'd use GPS, or failing that I'd use a compass and ground reference points.'

'I can teach you a few of the constellations, if you like,' he said.

'I'd like that,' she said. From the way he'd talked about the stars, this was clearly his passion, just like flying was hers. She was intrigued to see what made him tick.

He spread the blanket on the ground and set the cushions on one end. She lay down beside him, feeling ridiculously like a teenager.

And then the stars started coming into view.

'I don't really remember looking at the skies at night here when I was a child,' she said. 'We were usually in the villa, either under the blankets with Portia telling us stories by torchlight, or we were on the terrace with all the citronella candles. And you never see skies like this at home— the stars look so big and bright.'

'That's the benefit of no light pollution,' he said. 'See that kite shape up there?'

She squinted into the darkness. 'Yes.'

'That's Boötes,' he said. 'He's the hunter who follows the two bears, Ursa Major and Ursa Minor, around the pole—he was actually mentioned in Homer's *Odyssey*.'

'That star at the bottom is really bright,' she said.

'Arcturus, the bear guard. It's the fourth brightest in the sky,' he said, 'and is a hundred times brighter than our sun.'

'That's amazing,' she said. 'And yet it looks so tiny.'

'That's the difference between one hundred and fifty million kilometres and thirty-six light years,' he said. 'And next to Boötes is Ursa Major—the one you call the Big Dipper.'

'Up there.' She pointed to the seven stars she'd always seen as a bowl with a handle.

'Draw an imaginary line up through the right-hand side of the bowl, and you get to a really bright star.'

'I see it.'

'That's the top of the handle of the Little Dipper—Ursa Minor,' he said. 'And the bright star is Polaris.'

'The North Star,' she said.

He smiled. 'So you know more than you think about the stars. And see that W-shaped constellation up there?'

'I see it.'

'That's Cassiopeia. She was the wife of King Cepheus, and she boasted that she and her daughter Andromeda were more beautiful than the Nereids, the sea nymphs. They weren't very happy about it, so Poseidon sent Cetus, a sea monster, to terrorise them. Cassiopeia and Cepheus agreed to sacrifice Andromeda to the monster, but Perseus saved her. Some say that Cassiopeia hangs upside down in the sky as a reminder not to be boastful.'

'Quite a story,' she said.

'Perseus has his own constellation close by— and there's a meteor shower from there every summer.' He smiled. 'Andromeda's there, too. And Cetus the sea monster.'

'You're good at this,' she said. She remembered what Gloria had said about him turning down a place at Cambridge. 'Was it astronomy you were going to study at university?'

He groaned. 'Mum's been talking to you about that?'

'She mentioned it.'

He sighed. 'Look, it's not a big deal.'

'Turning down a place at Cambridge is a pretty big deal.'

'No, it isn't. Anyone else would've done the same in my shoes.'

'Would they?' she asked.

He blew out a breath. 'I have four younger sisters. Mum was crippled with arthritis. If I'd gone away to study, there's a good chance that the girls would've been taken into care. Lucy was thirteen, Annie was eleven, Sadie was nine and Jade was seven. So it was an easy choice to stay. I didn't want my family broken up.'

So he'd given up his dreams to look after them all?

As if the question had been written over her face, he said, 'It's fine. There are plenty of other people out there who can look at black holes, exoplanets and quantum mechanics. And I taught myself computer science. If I'd gone away to study astrophysics, I wouldn't have developed the voice-control system and the chances are that Mum would still be having to rely on other people to do practically everything for her. She hated losing her independence on days when the inflammation's really bad.'

'But you've given some of her independence back to her,' Immi pointed out. 'And now she's settled here. I'm guessing all your sisters are grown up and settled, too?'

'Yes. Lucy and her husband had a baby at Christmas, Annie got married in the spring, Sadie's in the middle of doing an MBA, and Jade's just qualified as a teacher.'

'So I'm guessing this is the crossroads you were talking about, the other night?'

'Mm.' His tone was noncommittal.

She winced. 'Sorry. I don't mean to sound as if I'm prying. I was just thinking, you helped me by listening, so maybe it's my turn to help you.'

He sighed. 'Mum's got this bee in her bonnet that I missed out on doing my degree. I've told her it doesn't worry me, but I know she feels it's her fault and she feels guilty about it.'

'Do you want to do a degree?' she asked.

'Maybe. Maybe not. I'm OK here.'

'Being OK isn't quite the same as following your heart and doing what you really want to do,' she said softly.

He was silent for so long that she thought she'd offended him. And then he blew out a breath. 'I've taken the voice-control system about as far as it can go—and my staff are all great, so the business practically runs itself. I need a challenge. But right now I'm not sure what. Part of me wants to go travelling—but I don't want to dump Mum's care onto someone else.'

'Does she see it that way?' Immi asked. 'I got the impression that she thinks she holds you back.'

He sighed. 'She wants to see me married with children.'

Immi went cold. That was a good reason to keep her distance from Matt—because she might not be able to have children. She'd read articles that said anorexia affected your fertility. Her periods had never been regular, and she'd stopped having periods for a year at the lowest point of her illness. But her family was worried enough about her, so she had always kept her fears locked inside, not even discussing it with her twin.

And now the issue had raised its ugly head again.

'Is that what you want?' she asked carefully.

'I'm not sure I want children at all to be honest.'

She could understand that—if he'd felt responsible for his sisters at such a young age, of course he'd be wary of having all that responsibility again.

'I haven't met the woman who made me want to settle down yet,' he added.

She reminded herself that that included her.

'And my dates don't tend to like the idea of me coming as a package. They expect me to dump Mum's care onto someone else and...' He grimaced. 'Sorry. That isn't very fair of me. Of course anyone would expect to come first in their partner's life.'

'Maybe there's scope for compromise, if you met The One?'

'Such as?'

'A family home with a granny annexe?' she suggested. 'So your mum's still got all her independence, but she's also living near enough for you not to worry about her.'

'I'm not sure there are many properties on the island that could be remodelled like that,' he said, 'and the climate here is better for Mum's health, so I don't want to drag her back to England.'

'Doesn't she get a say in it?'

He sighed. 'Of course she does. But I don't want her sacrificing her personal comfort for me. That wouldn't be fair.'

'I get where you're coming from, but I don't think she wants you to sacrifice yourself for her, either. And I'm also guessing that maybe now she's at the stage where she wants to see you as her son, not her carer.'

'I never thought of that.'

'It's something my best friend Lizzie's grand-mother said to her, when she went into sheltered housing. She didn't want Lizzie coming over with her shopping and running errands—she wanted to see her granddaughter and spend time with her. I'm guessing that's how your mum's starting to see things. So maybe you need to talk to her. And I mean honestly.'

'I guess.' He reached over and squeezed her hand. 'Thanks. You've given me something to think about.'

'Maybe,' she said, 'you could follow your dreams and go travelling. I don't mean anything like taking a complete gap year for a round-the-world trip or what have you, the way my parents just have, but just a few weeks. Perhaps you could come back for a couple of days mid-trip so you can reassure yourself that your mum's doing OK. That might be a good compromise for you both.'

'It probably would,' he agreed.

She noticed that he was still holding her hand; and she really ought to find a tactful way of removing her hand from his. Yet for the life of her she couldn't pull away, because she liked the feeling of his fingers tangled with hers.

They lay there in a strange companionable silence, just watching the stars, and Matt pointed out a couple more constellations. 'That one's Lupus, the wolf.'

She scoffed. 'It looks nothing like a wolf.'

He laughed. 'Hey, I wasn't the one who named them. Blame—well, nobody knows who was actually the first to name them, but the first written record of the names is from the Greek poet Aratus, nearly two and a half thousand years ago.'

'It still doesn't look like a wolf.'

They lay there until the air started to get chilly, and then Matt sighed. 'I guess we'd better get back.'

He saw her back to the house—and strangely they still seemed to be holding hands. This time, he kissed her on the cheek. 'Goodnight, Immi.'

Her skin tingled where his lips had touched her, and it was the easiest thing in the world to kiss his cheek back. Except somehow he'd moved and she ended up brushing her mouth against his. It felt as if she'd been galvanised. She felt him go very still, too. And then he dropped the blankets and cushions he'd been holding in his free hand, slid his arms round her and kissed her properly.

It felt as if she were floating among the stars they'd just been watching. And it had never been like this before when someone had kissed her—not Shaun, not the rare boyfriends she'd had at university, not Stephen.

He broke the kiss. 'I'm sorry. That wasn't meant to happen.'

She laid her palm against his cheek. 'It wasn't just you.'

'I've been wanting to do that since I first met you,' he admitted. 'The only reason I held back was that rock on your left hand.'

'Which isn't there any more,' she said softly.

He grimaced. 'This isn't fair of me—we're both at a crossroads and I shouldn't be making extra complications.'

'Or maybe,' she said, 'we can think of this as something out of time—a few snatched moments for you and me. No strings and no commitments.'

'No strings and no commitments,' he echoed, then shook his head. 'That feels a bit dishonourable.'

'I have no idea where my life is headed, so I can't offer you anything but the here and now,' she said, 'and I think right now you and I are both in the same boat.'

'So maybe we should travel along together while we're both here?'

'Something like that,' she said.

He kissed her again. 'Let's talk tomorrow—if we still feel the same, then it's a deal.'

A thrill of anticipation slid through her. She was pretty sure she'd still feel the same way tomorrow. But would he?

'Goodnight, sweet Imogen,' he said softly, and stole a last kiss.

'Goodnight, Matt.'

And, for the first time in months, as she went to bed Immi's heart felt light.

CHAPTER SIX

'GOOD AFTERNOON.'

The moment she heard Matt's voice, Immi looked up from where she was kneeling on the grass and hacking back more shrubbery. 'Good afternoon.' Then she realised what he was carrying. 'Why the bucket and the toolbox?' she asked.

'Cement,' he said. 'I'm going to make a start on repairing the crumbling bits of wall.'

She looked at him, alarmed. 'But is that safe?'

'I won't do anything dangerous,' he said. 'I promise.'

'OK.'

He said quietly, 'And we need to talk about last night.'

'Uh-huh.' Was this where he was going to suggest that they be sensible and pretend it had never happened—because they didn't have any kind of future?

'Have you had enough time to think about it?'

She really couldn't tell a thing from his expression. Did he have doubts? She stood up. 'Have you?'

'I asked first.' But there was a tiny quirk at the corner of his mouth. 'Yes. I've thought about it.'

'Remind me never to play poker with you,' she said dryly.

He laughed. 'I wasn't thinking about poker. I was thinking more of dinner tonight. There's a nice restaurant in the next village.'

And she didn't have the excuse that she only had casual clothes with her, because she had access to all Sofia's beautiful dresses. 'Are we talking posh or casual?'

'Would posh be a problem?' There was a tiny slash of colour across his cheeks. 'I remember the third time I saw you.'

'Third?'

'The first time, you were only interesting in

finding out what was going on with Andie,' he said. 'The second time, you were busy cutting flowers ready to arrange for the wedding.'

Now she understood. 'The third time was when I was Andie's bridesmaid.' When they'd danced together. When he'd almost kissed her. When she'd felt that incredible pull towards him— something that she shouldn't have felt.

But things were different now.

She was no longer engaged to Stephen.

She could acknowledge her feelings—and act on them.

'So you want me to wear that dress?'

'You wear,' he said, 'whatever you like.' He gave her another of those quirky smiles that made her feel as if her knees had just melted. 'But I thought you looked amazing in that teal mantua dress.'

He actually remembered what she'd called it? He'd paid that much attention to what she said? It warmed her all the way through. 'I'll see what I can do,' she said. 'What time?'

'I'll pick you up at seven?' he suggested.

'OK.'

He put the bucket and toolbox down, took her hand and drew it up to his mouth, then pressed a kiss into her palm and folded her fingers over it. 'You're going back to England at the end of the month and I might be going away, if things work out. So, just to make it clear, there aren't any strings to dinner.'

That sounded like his strong sense of honour talking. And although part of her appreciated it, part of her wanted something else entirely. 'What if I want there to be strings?'

He caught his breath. 'They'd be temporary strings.'

'A "helping each other over the crossroads" kind of thing,' she suggested. 'That works for me.'

His eyes were very dark. 'Are you sure about this?'

'Yes.' She paused. 'Are you?'

'Yes.' His voice seemed to have dropped an octave, all deep and husky and sexy. And it thrilled her that she could turn a clever man like Matthew Stark into mush.

Immi the Elephant.

She pushed the words away. Yes, she'd felt inadequate in the past, but that was then and this was now. She wasn't going to let the past derail her. She was going to have a mad fling with a gorgeous man—a fling with no consequences for either of them. And they were both going to enjoy it.

'Tonight,' she said, hearing the crack in her own voice.

'Tonight,' he echoed, and the heat in his expression made her blood sing.

Immi spent the rest of the afternoon working in the garden, and took a break partway through to take Matt a jug of iced water.

'This is wonderful—thank you,' he said.

She smiled at him. 'You're doing a great job of

repairing that wall.' He'd already repaired one crumbled section and was working on a second.

'It's probably not as straight as it should be,' he admitted, 'because someone might just have distracted me a bit, earlier.'

She rolled her eyes. 'Tsk. And you being a picky scientist, and all.'

He grinned back. 'How's the shrubbery-taming going?'

'It's getting there. I'm starting another pile of branches,' she said.

'Let me know if you need the shredder any sooner than next week.' He paused. 'I meant to ask you earlier—do you have any food allergies, and are you OK with fish?'

'Fish?' she queried.

'The place I have in mind tends to do a catch of the day—there isn't a written menu,' he said. 'You get what the chef bought fresh from the harbour that morning.'

'Fresh is good. Plus no menu saves being forced to choose between two things you really like the sound of,' she said with a smile. 'And no, I don't have any allergies or any strong dislikes.'

'Great.'

'I guess I'd better let you get back to your cement,' she said. 'See you later.'

Matt's car had gone from outside the house by the time Immi went back to the villa to get ready. She scrubbed away the gardening dirt in the bath and, with her wet hair wrapped in a towel, started looking through Sofia's wardrobe.

Funny, she felt as nervous as a teenager. Even though she knew Matt was one of the good guys, she felt a slight edge of anticipation about her date. What if it went wrong? What if he changed his mind?

What if it went right?

In some ways, that was more scary. She'd come to realise that one of the reasons she'd chosen Stephen was that he'd never really challenged her emotionally or sexually: he'd been safe. Whereas Matthew Stark was very different. She'd never felt this strong sensual pull to anyone before, and it scared her as much as it excited her.

Could she open up to him? Be her real self? Or would he think she was inadequate? She shook herself and picked out the teal dress she'd worn at the wedding. Luckily, she could remember Posy showing her the safe's combination for the costume jewellery, so she took out the pearl collar and the brooch she'd worn with it before. It didn't take long to do her hair and make-up, and she was ready at five minutes to seven.

At exactly seven, Matt turned up, wearing a dark suit, white shirt and an understated dark red tie.

'You look beautiful, Immi,' he said.

'Thank you.' She smiled. 'So do you.'

He raised an eyebrow. 'Can you call a man beautiful?'

She pressed her palm lightly against his cheek. 'I think so.'

'Why, thank you, Ms Marlowe.' He twisted his head so he could press a kiss into her palm, and it made her knees go weak. What would it be like when he kissed her later tonight, after dinner? Especially as they'd agreed that tonight was no strings... Her pulse sped up a notch.

'Ready to go?' he asked.

Not quite trusting herself to speak, she simply smiled and nodded.

He opened the car door for her, then drove them to the next village. To Immi's delight, the restaurant overlooked the sea and three of the walls were pure glass to take full advantage of the views. The tables were all set with pristine white damask cloths and silver cutlery, and there was a scented tea-light candle in the centre of each table, set in a black metal holder with cut-out stars. The whole place looked incredibly romantic—and seriously expensive.

'We're going halves, right?' she asked in a low voice.

'No. My idea, my bill,' he said.

'Only on condition,' she said, 'I get to have an idea and pick up a bill later in the week.'

He gave her a considering look. 'If you insist.'

'I do. It looks really busy, too.' And she'd just bet that you had to book this place weeks in advance. She narrowed her eyes suspiciously at him. 'How did you manage to get a table at the last minute?'

'The owner's mum is one of my mum's friends.'

She raised an eyebrow. 'Quite a network Gloria has.'

'My mother is an amazing networker. Actually, they're in the same book club, and Giovanna also walks with a stick.'

Then the penny dropped. 'And would I be right in guessing that you came up with a few things on one of your systems to make Giovanna's life easier?'

He shrugged. 'It's what I do.'

And, given that Gloria had told her Matt's system was expensive unless you were disabled, she'd also bet that he hadn't charged Giovanna a penny for setting up the system. Stephen would've been all about maximising profit, but

Matt had definite Robin Hood tendencies. She liked that. A man who cared and who tried to make a positive difference to the world by making other people's lives better.

A man came over and greeted Matt warmly with a kiss on both cheeks. 'Matteo, it's good to see you.'

'You, too, Carlo. Immi, this is Carlo Costaldo, owner of the restaurant. Carlo, this is my friend Imogen Marlowe,' Matt introduced them swiftly.

'My friends call me Immi,' she said, holding out her hand.

Carlo took it and shook it warmly. 'Then I hope I may call you Immi.'

'Of course.'

At her smile, Carlo took them to a table in the corner with an amazing view over the sea. 'Can I bring you some wine?' he asked.

'I'm driving,' Matt said, 'so I'll stick to still water, thanks.'

'Just one glass for me, please,' Immi said. 'What would you recommend?'

'We have a good Pinot Grigio,' Carlo said. 'It's from a local vineyard. The winemaker reserves his best wines for us.'

'Then that would be lovely.'

Carlo brought over a bottle of still mineral water and glasses for both of them, and a glass of wine for Immi.

'*Saluti,*' he said.

'*Saluti,*' she echoed and took a sip. 'This is perfect. Thank you.'

'*Prego.* Enjoy your meal,' Carlo said.

They had scampi in a cream sauce to start. 'This is the best scampi I've ever tasted,' Immi said.

'You never know what they're going to serve here,' Matt told her, 'but you can always be sure it's going to be superb. It's the best food on the island.'

The same was true of their next course: pasta with olives, chilli, and cherry tomatoes. 'It's pretty much the island's signature dish,' Matt explained.

It was followed by a whole white fish grilled with lemon and served with tiny new potatoes and garlicky spinach, and then a lemon and strawberry tiramisu. 'Oh, wow. The sponges have been soaked in *limoncello*. Sofia would've loved this,' Immi said. And how good it felt that she could enjoy this, instead of mentally working out every gram of fat and every calorie she was consuming.

Finally they sat drinking coffee and nibbling tiny *amaretti* biscuits. Immi could see the harbour lights twinkling in the port opposite, and there was a silver path of moonlight on the sea. The view was unbelievably romantic; and Matt clearly thought so, too, because he reached over the table to hold her hand.

'OK?' he asked.

'Very OK,' she said. 'I don't think I've ever been anywhere so lovely.'

'I'm glad,' he said softly.

Once he'd paid the bill, he drove them back to the villa. Immi caught her breath as she opened the gate and saw that the terrace was all lit up with fairy lights. The garden looked magical; and the scent of the honeysuckle and the jasmine perfumed the air.

'How did...?' She looked at Matt, pretty sure that he was the one behind this. 'When did you do this?'

'This afternoon. Just before I came to talk to you,' he admitted.

'What if I'd said I'd changed my mind?'

He shrugged. 'Then you could've just enjoyed the fairy lights anyway. I did say there were no strings.'

'This is just...' She gave a sigh of pleasure. 'It's lovely, Matt.'

'The lights are solar-powered,' he said, 'so you don't have to worry about maintenance—and if Posy hates them, it's easy enough to get rid of them or put them somewhere else in the garden, if she prefers.'

'Oh, I think she'll keep them,' Immi said.

He smiled. 'Dance with me?'

'I'd love to.'

He took his smartphone from his pocket and placed it on the table. One click later, and she recognised the opening bars of 'Wonderful Tonight'.

'I picked the song deliberately,' he said, 'because you do.'

And he wasn't being cheesy or spinning her a line; the expression in his eyes was utterly sincere.

'Thank you.' She smiled. 'You know we're being a terrible cliché here—the best man and the bridesmaid.'

He smiled back and drew her into his arms. 'Works for me.'

Just like last time, they were dancing under the stars, in the garden that overlooked the sea, with the air full of the scent of summer flowers.

Just like last time, she tingled where he touched her.

Just like last time, she found herself staring at

his mouth—then glancing up and realising that he was staring at her mouth, too.

Except this time was different. This time, he didn't back away or make an excuse. This time, he simply dipped his head to hers and kissed her, his mouth warm and sweet, asking rather than demanding.

And this time, she kissed him all the way back.

This was everything she'd dreamed it would be. Everything she wanted.

She had no idea how long they stood there, swaying to the music and kissing. She couldn't even remember what songs had played; all she could think about was the way he made her feel. Special. Wanted. Adored.

'I remember the last time we danced.' His voice was low and husky with desire.

'So do I.'

'When I first saw you in that dress, I wanted to untie that bow.'

She smiled. 'Then do it.'

'Sure?'

'Very sure—though maybe not in the middle of the terrace.' She knew the garden was private and nothing overlooked it, but even so she took his hand and led him through the house to the bedroom.

Strange. She'd never really been this assertive in her relationships before. She'd always held back, unsure of herself. But Matt made her feel confident. The heat in his expression told her how much he wanted her, and it gave her a heady feeling.

He gently removed the brooch from the middle of the bow at the front of the dress. 'Oh—it doesn't actually untie,' he said, sounding disappointed.

She turned round. 'There's a zip.'

'Good,' he said, and bent forward to kiss the nape of her neck just beneath the pearl collar before sliding the zip all the way down.

She stepped out of the dress. 'Matt, I know it's fussy of me—'

'—but that's vintage high-end couture. It needs

hanging up properly,' he finished. 'You're not being fussy. You're being careful of someone else's things. There's a difference.'

She put the dress on its hanger and put it away in the wardrobe.

Then it struck her that he was fully dressed, and she was in her underwear. 'Matt.' She looked at him. 'You're wearing, um, too much.'

He slid his jacket off and hung it over the back of a chair. 'Better?'

'Not quite.'

He gave her a wicked grin and removed his tie. 'Now?'

She gave the tiniest shake of her head, and he laughed and spread his hands. 'How about I leave it to you?'

He was putting her in control of the pace, and her hands were actually shaking as she unbuttoned his shirt and slid the soft cotton over his shoulders. Even though she'd seen him shirtless before, when he'd been painting the wall while wearing nothing but a pair of shorts, this was different. Because this time she was undressing him with intent.

She made an effort to sound casually appreciative. 'Nice musculature, Mr Stark.'

'Why, thank you, Ms Marlowe.' He dipped his head and kissed her. 'And now I think you're wearing too much.' He slid his palms up her spine, and she could barely breathe when his fingers went to the catch of her bra.

But then her old insecurities slammed in. It must have shown on her face, because he stopped. 'Immi? What's wrong?'

'It's not you,' she said. 'And it's a long and boring story.' She dragged in a breath. 'I, um, had a few body issues as a teen.'

His dark eyes were full of understanding. 'A lot of teens do. There's so much pressure on girls to look a certain way.' He rested his palm against her cheek. 'If we're taking this too fast, we can stop.'

It would be the easy way out. And she knew she would regret it. She wanted Matt. 'I don't want to stop.'

'But?'

'I'm scared,' she admitted. 'Scared that I won't be enough.'

'Come with me,' he said softly, and drew her over to the chevalier mirror in the corner of the room.

A mirror. The thing she'd avoided so often as a teen.

Immi the Elephant.

He stood behind her. 'I want you to see what I see,' he said. 'I see a strong, beautiful woman. I see beautiful hazel eyes. A mouth that makes me ache to taste it.' He rubbed the pad of his thumb against her lower lip. 'I see the curve of a neck that makes me want to kiss it.' He dipped his head to press a kiss against the curve of her neck. 'I see curves. Beautiful curves. And that's not a euphemism for fat.' He drew his hands down her sides, moulding her curves. 'I see a woman who makes my heart beat faster. A woman I find really attractive. A woman I want to make love with.' He kissed the nape of her neck. 'You're enough, Immi. You're what I want. But only if you want this, too.'

She could see it in his eyes. He was being absolutely sincere. And when he drew her back against his body, she could feel the evidence of his desire pressing against her.

You're enough.

Those two words, quietly spoken, seeped through the panic. He meant it. He wanted her as much as she wanted him.

She turned to face him. 'I want you, too, Matt.'

'Sure?'

'Sure.' She swallowed hard. 'But you're still overdressed. You need to lose the trousers.'

'Trousers. Right.' He held her gaze and removed his trousers.

Her heart sped up a notch. This was really happening.

'Now,' he said softly, and slid his palms up her spine again. This time, she made no protest as he undid the catch of her bra and let her breasts spill into his hands. 'You're beautiful, Immi. I ache for you,' he said.

'Me, too,' she said, her voice cracking.

After that, she wasn't sure which of them finished undressing each other, but the next thing she knew he'd picked her up and laid her on the bed.

'If you want me to stop,' he said softly, 'it's not too late to change your mind.'

It was way too late for that. She wanted him like she'd never wanted anyone before. 'I want you to stay,' she said.

'With pleasure,' he said, and climbed onto the bed next to her.

Feeling his skin against hers made her catch her breath. The warmth of his body. The beat of his heart. The feeling of completion as he gently eased inside her.

Making love with him was like nothing she'd ever experienced before. Every touch, every kiss, made her feel warm and cherished and desired for herself. They were making love together be-

cause they wanted to—not because an immature teenage boy had made a bet with his equally
immature friends, or because she was the boss's
daughter and he saw her as a stepping stone for
his ambition.

They were making love because they were at-
tracted to each other.

Because they actually *liked* each other.

Their first time should've been awkward and
embarrassing and just not quite right; instead, to
Immi's surprise, it was perfect. As if they'd always known each other, as if they already knew
exactly how and where each other liked being
kissed and touched. And she was shocked and
thrilled in equal measure when Matt found new
places that made her gasp with pleasure—places
she'd never thought might be an erogenous zone,
but the touch of Matt's mouth and Matt's hands
suddenly made them one.

Afterwards, when Matt had dealt with the con-
dom in the bathroom, he came back to hold

her and they snuggled close together under the sheets.

He kissed the top of her head. 'I feel so bad that I can't stay tonight.'

'Of course you can't stay,' she said softly. 'If your mum needed you she wouldn't be able to contact you.'

'It's just—well, I'm not in the habit of making love with someone and then walking away, as if it didn't matter.'

'You don't have to feel guilty, Matt,' she said. 'We agreed this is a temporary thing so all the rules are different, and anyway I understand the situation—you're not going because you're a selfish user who doesn't give a damn about how I feel. You're going because you're needed elsewhere, and that's OK by me.'

'Thank you.' He kissed her again. 'Tomorrow was supposed to be your wedding day, wasn't it?'

The day that would've seen her making the worst mistake of her life. 'Yes.'

'Are any of your sisters coming over to be with you?'

'No. They offered,' she said, 'but I want Andie to concentrate on her pregnancy and Portia to enjoy being a newlywed. And Posy's really busy. I don't want her to drop everything for me. Mum has enough on her hands with Dad.'

He stole a kiss. 'Putting your family before your own needs?'

'Pots and kettles,' she said, kissing him back.

'Then if you're going to be on your own,' he said, 'come and play tourist with me.'

'Tourist?'

'L'Isola dei Fiori is full of hidden little corners,' he said. 'Let's go and explore them.'

'Taking my mind off the might-have-beens?' she asked.

'That, too.'

'I've never actually played tourist,' she admitted. 'When we stayed here as children, we always hung round the villa, the garden or the beach. I've been to San Rocco a couple of times, but that's about it.'

'Good. We'll have fun. I'll pick you up at about eight and we can have breakfast out.'

'Provided you let me buy breakfast,' she said.

'Deal,' he said, and kissed her again. 'The dress code tomorrow is casual, stuff you might not mind getting messy, plus a swimming costume—oh, and sturdy shoes you can wear on a beach.'

'Messy? And why would you need shoes on a beach?'

He refused to be drawn. 'Wait and see.'

He climbed out of bed; she stayed where she was, propping herself up on one elbow while she watched him get dressed.

'I feel as if I ought to be playing the opposite of music to strip to—though I'm not quite sure what that is,' he teased.

She started to hum, 'You can leave your hat on,' and he laughed.

'I don't think that quite works, Immi.' He came

over to the bed and kissed her lingeringly. 'You look comfortable. Stay there—I'll make sure I lock the door behind me.'

'OK.'

'Sweet dreams,' he said softly.

Oh, they would be. Because they'd be of him.

Immi lay there in the soft lamplight, thinking how good tonight had been and how glad she was that she'd met Matt. He was definitely helping her through her personal crossroads; right at that moment she felt better about herself than she had in a long, long time.

She just hoped she could do the same for him.

And as for what happened at the end of her month in L'Isola dei Fiori… She'd leave that to sort itself out. For once in her life she wasn't going to plan. She was just going to let it happen.

The next morning, she was ready at eight.

'Is this OK?' she asked when Matt arrived to collect her, gesturing to her shorts and T-shirt.

'Absolutely fine.' He looked at her feet. 'And canvas shoes. Perfect.'

'Why would you need shoes on a beach?' she asked again.

'So you really don't know the island that well, then?' He grinned. 'You're going to love this.'

'If you're going to be irritating and do the whole "wait and see" bit, then I'll pretend to be all my sisters and me at the age of four,' she threatened.

'Ah. I remember that stage with my own sisters. I had *years* of it.' He adopted a falsetto voice. '"Are we there, yet?"—repeated ad nauseam.'

She laughed. 'Got it.'

'OK. We're going to the south of the island,' he said, 'and we're starting at a little fishing village where apparently the pastries have to be tasted to be believed. And then we're going to do something that's been done here for at least two thousand years. That's the messy bit.'

'Now I'm intrigued,' she said.

But she was prevented from saying more by a barrage of beeps from her phone.

'Your sisters?' he asked.

'And my mum.' She sighed. 'Do you mind if I'm horribly rude and text them back, so I can reassure them that I'm not moping around?'

'Sure,' he said.

She read the texts, and typed swiftly into her phone.

Am fine. *Really* fine. I miss you, but I'm fine. Am spending today doing touristy things and having fun. It's going to be a good day. Love you.

She sent the text to her mother and her sisters, then switched her phone to silent. 'They'll think I'm back at the villa and out of range if I don't answer,' she said.

'It's fine, Immi. It's natural for your family to worry about you in the circumstances. I'd be more worried for you if they didn't.'

She gave him a rueful smile. 'I guess. I'm lucky. My family's brilliant.'

He parked the car in the village and they walked to the seafront. Just as he'd promised, the *pasticceria* had an amazing array of pastries.

'What do you recommend?' she asked.

'The island's speciality is *sfogliatelle*,' he said. 'They're flaky pastries filled with orange-flavoured ricotta.'

At one time she would've found an excuse not to have them. Even with Stephen, she'd found herself being careful what she ate. But with Matt she could relax and enjoy new tastes, new sensations. 'Sounds good—I think I'll try them. What are you having?'

'The same,' he said.

She ordered two pastries, a cappuccino for herself and an espresso for Matt, and they ate on the terrace outside the *pasticceria*, overlooking the jetty and watching the boats. 'This is so pretty,' she said, and took a snap of the view on her phone.

Having sfogliatelle for breakfast at the pastry

shop. This is the view, she typed, and sent the picture to her mother and sisters.

They had a stroll down the jetty after breakfast, and then Matt drove them down a narrow road to what looked like a gorge.

'We're going for a walk?' she guessed.

'No. This is the messy bit.'

'And two thousand years old, you said earlier. Nope. I still don't get it,' she said.

'Then come with me,' he said, and led her deeper into the narrow gorge. 'It's the original Roman baths,' he said.

'Seriously? We're actually allowed to use them?'

'We are indeed,' he said. 'There's also a natural sauna here—a cave with stone benches carved into the rock, and it gets pretty hot there.'

'So you've been here before?' she asked.

'Nope. I found the details in a tourist guidebook,' he confessed with a smile. 'But I thought it sounded great. Apparently you can be painted with mud, sit in the sun until it sets, then wash it off and your skin will be super-soft.'

'Now I get what you meant about messy.' She grinned back. 'This is brilliant. Thank you, Matt. I can't think of anyone I'd rather share this with.'

'Me, too.' He tightened his fingers round hers. 'I had a feeling you might have a sense of adventure and you'd enjoy exploring.'

And in that moment Immi had a real idea of what was going on in Matt's head. Why he felt stuck. He had a sense of adventure and wanted to explore—yet he was here on a tiny Mediterranean island with his disabled mother, putting her needs first.

He wasn't a martyr—he clearly loved Gloria and he didn't begrudge the fact that he was looking after her. But he clearly couldn't see a way of making it work so he could keep looking after his mother and explore the world at the same time.

She really hoped he was thinking about what she'd told him about her friend's experience and was planning to talk to Gloria. She was pretty sure that his mother would be understanding.

'Stone pillows?' she asked as they were shown into one of the caves. 'Oh, and there's a little dent in them where people over the years have lain there—that's amazing.'

Lying in the warm water was incredibly relaxing; and the mud treatment turned out to be fun, particularly when their therapist let them paint each other with the mud. Immi couldn't resist dabbing mud on the end of Matt's nose. By the time he'd retaliated and it had turned into a full-on mud fight, they were both covered.

They sat in the sun, drinking cold sparkling water, and waited for the mud to set. 'I didn't think it'd take quite this long to get rid of the mud,' she said ruefully in the shower when they were rinsing off the mud. 'But I still can't get my head round the fact we're showering in naturally warm water.'

'It's amazing, isn't it?' He smiled at her. 'Let me do your back.'

His touch was firm, yet gentle; and Immi had flashbacks to the way his hands had made her feel, the previous night. When she turned to face him, she could tell by his expression that he'd been thinking the same. 'I'll do your back,' she said, slightly embarrassed by the fact that her voice had gone all low and gravelly. And cleaning the mud off his skin was a great excuse to explore all the muscles on his back. Matt Stark was definitely one of the most gorgeous men she'd ever seen.

After lunch, Matt took her to another beach. 'This one's perfect for beach combing and rock pools,' he said.

'And I need shoes?'

'Not for this one—that's later,' he said.

Immi walked hand in hand with him along the shoreline, and was delighted to discover tiny fish, yellow and orange crabs, and translucent shrimps among the rock pools. And the beach itself yielded treasure: small pieces of white and blue and green sea glass, mosaic tiles, and pebbles that had been washed smooth among the tumble of the waves. She sneaked one into the pocket of her cut-off jeans, wanting a memory of the day to keep.

Finally, he took her to the beach he'd told her about.

She read the warning notices at the top of the path that led to the beach. 'The sand is a hundred degrees?' She looked at him, shocked.

'Remember, the island's on a volcanic ridge,' he said. 'Normally, when you dig down into sand it gets cooler; here, it gets hotter, because of the fumaroles.'

'Fumarole?'

'A vent of hot volcanic gas,' he said. 'And the restaurant where we're eating uses the beach to cook our food. Let's go and choose dinner—it takes about an hour and a half.'

'This,' she said, 'is the most unusual thing I've ever done.'

'Good. I wanted to give you a day to remember for all the right reasons.'

'You've certainly done that,' she said.

They both chose chicken, and Immi watched,

fascinated, as the chef wrapped chicken, tomatoes, wine and rosemary in foil, then in a layer of cloth. 'It keeps the sand out, and the scent of the herbs in,' the chef explained.

And then she watched as the *maître d'* dug through the grey-brown layer at the top of the beach; she could see the steam rising from the black sand underneath.

'Is it OK to take a photograph?' she asked.

'Sure,' the *maître d'* said.

She took a snap and watched him bury the foil and cloth parcels under layers of sand, leaving a marker above them saying *'Stark'*. 'That's so cool,' she whispered to Matt, who smiled and stole a kiss.

'Your table will be ready in an hour,' the *maître d'* said with a smile.

'So we get to walk on the beach now?' Immi asked Matt.

'Yes, but tell me when it starts getting uncomfortable and we'll head back,' he said.

She could feel the heat of the sand through the

soles of her canvas shoes. 'So is the sea really warm here, too?' she asked.

'There are some hot springs a little further round the bay,' he said. 'We probably don't have time before dinner.'

'That's fine—I was just curious,' she said. 'And, actually, I think I'd rather get off the sand.'

'Let's go and have a drink,' he suggested.

Immi made sure to take photographs of every course: the antipasti of Parma ham and marinated artichokes; the thick spaghetti served with cheese and black pepper; and then the foil and cloth packets as they were retrieved from the beach, and then opened at their table to reveal perfectly cooked chicken with the scent of the wine, tomatoes and rosemary scenting the air.

'That's stunning,' she said, and sent the photographs to her mother and her sisters. 'And these will stop them all worrying about me.'

'Because of what today is?' Matt asked gently.

Oh, help. She'd almost let it slip about her old

eating disorder. 'Something like that,' she said, fudging the issue.

What she hadn't expected was the barrage of texts asking who she was with.

No texts until after dinner, she typed firmly, and switched her phone back to silent.

But when they were drinking coffee, she texted back.

A kind neighbour is keeping me company.

Glad you're not alone, Posy texted.

Matt's a really nice guy, Andie commented.

Matthew Stark is very easy on the eye. Could've been a model, was Portia's take on it.

Even though Immi hadn't mentioned his name, her twin and her older sister had clearly guessed who was keeping her company—and were making assumptions. Worse still, they were absolutely right.

She switched off her phone again, and Matt drove them back to the villa.

'Can I talk you into sharing a bottle of wine with me tonight?' she asked.

He thought about it for a moment. 'Sure. I could leave the car here tonight and walk home.'

'I thought bubbles,' she said. 'Is that OK with you?'

'Fine. Do you want me to open the bottle?'

'It's fine—I can manage,' she said with a smile. 'Go and sit on the terrace.'

When she went out again, carrying a bottle of chilled sparkling wine and two glasses, the fairy lights had come on and Matt was sitting on the wrought-iron bench with his eyes closed.

'Not watching the stars?' she asked lightly.

'No. I was concentrating on the scent of the flowers.'

'Jasmine and honeysuckle,' she said. 'The scent's stronger at night to attract the moths that pollinate them.'

'Makes sense.'

She poured the wine, and handed him a glass. 'Here's to making the right decisions,' she said. 'And to helping each other over a crossroads.'

'The right decisions and helping each other over a crossroads,' he echoed, clinking his glass against hers.

She sat down next to him, and he took her hand. 'I enjoyed today.'

'Me, too. It was a much, much better day than I was expecting—and it's all thanks to you. I appreciate that.'

'My pleasure.' He kissed her lightly. 'And I'm glad you didn't marry him. Not just for the purely selfish reason that it means I get to date you, but because you deserved more than he was offering you.' He wrinkled his nose. 'Not that I'm in a place to offer you anything. But you deserve better than that.'

'I'm not asking for more than these few days,' she said softly. 'That's enough for me. The here and now.'

'I wish I could stay tonight,' he said. 'I should've arranged for someone to come and stay with Mum.'

'It's fine,' she said. 'I'm not going to sit here

crying my eyes out, all maudlin and sad, think-ing of the might-have-beens. Because of you, I've had more fun today than I've had in months—I've been to new places, tried new things, and felt connected to the ancient Romans.'

He smiled. 'You'd look great in a toga.'

'Yeah, yeah.' She smiled back.

'And I'd have a lot of fun unwrapping you,' he said.

'Wait a second,' she said, and disappeared back into the villa.

It took a bit more than a second but, when Immi returned to the terrace, she was wrapped in a sheet.

'It's a bit ad hoc,' she said apologetically.

Matt laughed. 'Works for me.' His voice went suddenly deeper. 'So is that an invitation, Imo-gen Marlowe?'

'For you to unwrap me and have your wicked way with me, like an ancient Roman?' She wrin-kled her nose at him. 'I think it might be.'

'Accepted with pleasure,' he said, and did exactly what she'd suggested.

They drank the rest of the wine in bed, and then Matt kissed her. 'I'm sorry I can't stay tonight. But maybe we could sort something out for next weekend, or the weekend after. We could spend the day in San Rocco.' He paused. 'And maybe we can stay overnight.'

'I'd like that.'

He stole a kiss. 'See you tomorrow.'

'Tomorrow,' she said.

CHAPTER SEVEN

THE NEXT MORNING, Matt dropped by the kitchen before he collected his car. 'I thought you might like some pastries for breakfast,' he said.

'Thank you. Do you have time to share them with me?' she asked.

He glanced at his watch. 'Unfortunately not—and I'm afraid I won't get a chance to see you today. I promised to take Mum to see a friend on the mainland, and we're not going to be back until really late.'

She smiled. 'You don't need to explain, Matt. I don't expect you to spend every second of the day with me.'

He kissed her lightly. 'Thank you for under-standing.'

It sounded as if he'd dated needy, selfish women

in the past. Not that she could talk: she'd man-aged to pick really selfish men.

'I enjoyed yesterday,' she said.

'Me, too.'

She held his gaze. 'And I have no regrets. At all.'

'Good.' He kissed her again.

'I'm honestly fine, Matt. You don't need to treat me as if I'm made of glass. I won't break.'

'I know.' He stole a last kiss. 'Later. And that's a promise.'

Immi spent the day working in the garden, took a mid-afternoon paddle in the sea, and then walked down the hill so she could send her usual text to her mum and sisters to reassure them.

She added an extra text to Andie.

When Cleve flew his jet here where did he land?

The response came almost immediately.

Local flying club. Why?

Need a plane fix.

This time, the reply was a smiley face and a promise.

I'll see what I can find out.

It wasn't long before Andie sent another text with a contact name and number for the flying club.

You're really all right, Immi?

I'm really all right. I promise, she texted back.

So you and Matt...?

She could ignore the question. Or be honest—which would probably worry Andie. Maybe it was best to tell just part of the truth.

We're friends.

Her sister didn't need to know about the lovers bit.

He's a nice guy.

And that bit was definitely true.

* * *

On Monday morning, Immi called in to see Gloria, bringing her an armful of roses.

'These are gorgeous—though I feel a bit guilty that you're stripping the garden for me,' Gloria said with a rueful smile.

Immi laughed. 'I'm hardly stripping the garden. I need to cut the climbers back a bit, so really you're doing me a favour by taking the roses off my hands.'

'The real thanks I owe you is for Matt,' Gloria said. 'He actually talked to me yesterday.' She bit her lip. 'I've felt so guilty all these years that he's missed out on university because he looked after me and put me and the girls first. I did try to persuade him to go to university as a mature student, but he said it would feel like a backward step after developing his voice-control system and running the business.'

'And he loves you,' Immi added.

'He says he doesn't want to dump me in residential care.' Gloria sighed. 'He's got an overdeveloped sense of responsibility, because he had to pick up the reins at such a young age. But yesterday he told me that he'd like to go travelling. He asked me how I would feel about having a live-in companion for a month or so. And of course I don't mind. I just want to see him happy.' She looked at Immi. 'He said he'd been talking to you.'

'A bit,' Immi hedged, not wanting to break any confidences. Again, she wondered why Matt's father hadn't helped, but it felt too intrusive to ask. Instead, she said, 'I just told him about my best friend's grandmother—which isn't me calling you ancient, by the way, just telling him about a similar situation—and I told him he ought to talk to you. Obviously he thought about it and came to his own decision.'

'He wouldn't have thought about it at all if you hadn't talked to him.'

'Sometimes it's easier to see a solution from the outside,' Immi said. 'And I'm glad he's making plans.' Though she wasn't going to admit that she wished there might have been space for her in those plans. She and Matt had agreed that their fling was temporary. Wanting more would be greedy.

Matt was still in his office when Immi had finished her coffee and was ready to go back to the villa. 'I won't disturb him,' she said. 'Say hello to him for me.'

'I will,' Gloria promised. 'See you soon. And thanks again—for the flowers and for getting Matt to think about things.'

Later that afternoon, Matt went to the villa to see Immi. 'It was nice of you to call on Mum this morning.'

'It wasn't a duty visit. I like your mother very much and I enjoy spending time with her,' Immi told him.

'She loved the flowers.'

'Good.' She smiled at him. 'I was wondering, how are you in planes?'

'Planes?' He frowned, not having a clue what she meant.

'Flying in little planes,' she clarified. 'Two- or four-seaters.'

'I've never flown in anything that small. Why?'

'Apparently there's a flying club on the island. I need a flying fix, so I was considering seeing if I could rent a plane for an hour or so,' she said, 'and I wondered if you'd like to come with me—we could see the whole of L'Isola dei Fiori from the air.'

'I'd love to,' he said.

'Good. I'll let you know when I manage to sort something out. Are there any particular times I should avoid?'

'No, my diary's pretty flexible and I can move things if you need me to,' he said.

'OK. I'll book something and let you know the times.'

'And I wanted to say thank you,' he said. 'I had a long talk with Mum. You were right. She needs me to back off a bit and be her son, not her carer.'

'I'm glad you talked,' she said. 'So does this mean you're going travelling?'

'I want to be happy that everything's in place first—that she has a companion and a good support team while I'm not here. I've talked to my sisters, too, and they're happy about it. So I'm going away at the end of the month—and while I'm away maybe I'll work out what I want to do next.'

'That's good.' She paused. 'So where are you planning to go?'

'I have no idea.' He'd suppressed the longing for years and years, not wanting to frustrate himself by thinking of the places he'd love to go to but couldn't, because either the climate would be unbearable for his mother or the terrain wasn't wheelchair-friendly.

She blinked. 'There's a whole world out there, Matt—are you seriously telling me you can't think where to go?'

He threw the question back at her. 'Where would you go?'

'This time of year, probably Australia,' she said. 'It's the middle of their winter, so the temperature's bearable, and I'd go and see Uluru.'

'The stars are meant to be amazing in the Outback,' he said.

'Given how much you love astronomy,' she said thoughtfully, 'maybe you could do a tour with a difference and visit all the big telescopes.'

He smiled. 'Most of the arrays aren't actually open to the public—you need to be an academic with a good reason to visit.'

'All right—the observatories that are open to the public, then,' she amended.

'It's a thought,' he said. One that really appealed to him. And he was very tempted to ask her to come with him—to extend their fling just a little longer and share some adventures with him. 'Where else would you go, if you could go anywhere in the world?'

'At this time of year, Northern Europe's wonderful: the land of the midnight sun. I'd love to go to Svalbard and see the polar bears, and go whale-watching—better still if I can go in a small plane and follow the pod.'

'Is that where you were…?' He stopped. 'Sorry. I shouldn't ask. That's intrusive.'

'Going on honeymoon?' she guessed. 'No. Stephen wanted to go to the Caribbean.'

'You don't sound so keen.'

She shrugged. 'He thought it was romantic.'

'And you don't?' That was intriguing. Wasn't a Caribbean island, with its sunshine and white sand, meant to be where everyone would want to honeymoon? He couldn't help asking, 'What's your idea of romantic?'

'Fairy lights,' she said with a smile.

Exactly what he'd arranged on the terrace at the villa, the first time they'd made love.

'And gardens with amazing flowers, and the sea, and flying.'

'Maybe he'd arranged something like that for you as a surprise?'

She shook her head. 'When I cancelled the honeymoon, the travel agent didn't say a word about extras.' She shrugged. 'But it's all academic now, because I'm not going on honeymoon.'

'Is the garden giving you the space to think?' he asked.

'Some,' she said, 'but that's why I'm hoping to rent a plane. Flying crystallises a lot of things for me.'

'Like the stars do for me.'

She looked at him. 'Then maybe we need to follow our hearts, Matt—me with flying and you with the stars.'

'Maybe.' He sighed. 'I know I need to take a step back. But it's hard to trust someone else to do something I've spent half my life doing.' He grimaced. 'I need to stop being such a control freak.'

'I don't think it's being a control freak,' she said, 'as much as learning to trust that you can actually rely on someone else.' She squeezed his hand. 'If it helps, I find that hard, too. My sisters—well, that's different. We've always had each other's backs. But other people...'

'Maybe we can teach each other to trust,' Matt said slowly.

In the three weeks they had together? Immi wasn't so sure. But Matt had said nothing about changing the terms of their agreement. In three weeks' time, they might never see each other again. 'Perhaps,' she said carefully.

On Tuesday evening, they went for a walk on the beach before dinner.

As they wandered barefoot on the shoreline, hand in hand, Immi asked, 'Can I ask you something intrusive?'

Matt gave her a wary look. 'What?'

She decided to risk it. He could always change the subject if he didn't want to tell her, and she'd back off. 'I was wondering why you're the one who ended up as your mum's carer.'

'That's an easy one—I'm the oldest.'

She frowned. 'No, I mean… If my mum had been ill, Dad would've been the one to care for her, not Portia as the oldest daughter.'

'Your dad,' Matt said quietly, 'is an honour-able man.'

Which sounded as if his own father hadn't been. She said nothing, not wanting to stamp on a sore spot, and eventually he sighed. 'It's a messy story and it doesn't show anyone in a good light.'

'You don't have to tell me,' she said.

'Actually,' he said, 'you're the one who'll prob-ably understand. And I know you're not going to tell anyone.'

'Of course I'm not.'

'Mum started to get ill when I was twelve. I no-ticed that sometimes she had problems walking, and sometimes she found it difficult to mark her students' essays because her hand would cramp up.'

'So your mum was a teacher?'

'Modern languages,' he said. 'But when she had a flare-up there was no way she could sit or stand at school, so she had to give it up. She's done some translation work ever since, and she has a speech-to-text program on the computer so if she gets a flare-up she can still work—otherwise she'd hate feeling so helpless.'

'I know exactly where she's coming from,' Immi said. She'd hated the months in rehab, where it had felt as if everyone in her family treated her as a special case who needed constant cosseting. 'Did your dad teach, too?'

'No, he was a mechanic.' Matt grimaced. 'He was still of the generation that believed women should do all the housework and cooking, even if they worked full-time as well. So he wasn't very happy when Mum started to get ill and needed him to do things around the house that she couldn't manage.'

Immi's own father wasn't brilliant on the domestic front, but he had at least hired someone to do the cleaning and they'd all mucked in with laundry, cooking and any other chores that had come up.

'He decided he couldn't cope and left us the week after my fifteenth birthday,' Matt said. 'Not that he bothered telling any of us except Mum. He didn't even say goodbye.'

Immi was truly shocked. Despite his faults, Paul Marlowe would never have abandoned his wife. He loved all his daughters dearly, and he'd never dream of hurting them by walking out without a word. She winced. 'That's rough.'

'The girls thought it was their fault he left. I hated to see them breaking their hearts over it. So I went to see him at work at the garage, after school,' he said. 'I asked him why he wasn't coming home and why he hadn't said goodbye.' He paused. 'He said it was because it would've upset him too much.'

What about how his wife and children felt? Immi thought indignantly, but held the words back. Right now Matt needed her to listen, not judge.

'And then this woman came into the garage,' Matt said. 'She didn't even look at me; she only had eyes for him. She put her arms round him and kissed him—and that's when I knew. He'd been cheating on my mum for I don't know how long, and he was using her illness as his excuse to leave her for this other woman, while dumping all the blame on Mum.'

She tightened her hand round his, not knowing what to say, but wanting him to know that she was completely on his side.

'That's when I lost my temper and hit him,' he said. 'Just once. I found out later that I, um, broke his nose. She screamed a lot and said she was going to call the police. I told her to go ahead. I said that he was a liar and a coward—and if she had kids with him and anything went wrong, he'd cheat on her and dump them all, just as he had with my mum, me and my four sisters. I said I wished her luck with him because she'd really need it. And I told him I never wanted to see him again.'

'I'm sorry you had to go through that, Matt. And I don't blame you for punching him.'

'I'm not proud of myself,' Matt said. 'Violence doesn't solve anything. I bruised my hand so badly I couldn't write in my mock exams. Luckily my form teacher was brilliant and put in a word for me. And she helped with social services.'

'I'm glad you had someone who could help.' But what about his grandparents? Hadn't they stepped in to help?

As if the question had been written all over her face, he said, 'My father's parents took the attitude that men will be men. But that's not acceptable behaviour for any man. Or any woman, come to that. Lying and cheating... Just no.' Then he grimaced and squeezed her hand. 'Sorry. I know you've kind of been in my mum's position, being cheated on. I didn't mean to bring back bad memories for you.'

'My situation was nowhere near as bad. I don't have to cope with a debilitating illness and I don't have children to worry about.' She blew out a breath. 'You and your mum are truly amazing.'

He brushed the praise aside. 'Anyone would have done the same in my place.'

'I would definitely have wanted to punch your dad,' she said. 'Actually, I'd quite like to do that right now.'

He smiled, but his dark eyes were filled with sadness. 'As I said, violence doesn't solve anything, Immi. Punching him made me feel better for about thirty seconds—but it didn't change the situation at all.'

'Did you ever see him again?'

'Once.' He paused. 'Mum divorced him on the grounds of adultery and desertion. But he never paid her a penny in maintenance and he never sent any of us a birthday card or Christmas card.'

Immi was too shocked to say a word. How could anyone completely ignore his children like that?

'And then, once my voice-control system came out, there were a few newspaper articles about me. One of them reported that I was worth rather a lot of money at a very young age.'

She didn't like where this was heading. Matt's father had washed his hands of his wife and all his children when it suited him. Had he decided that he wanted to know Matt again solely because he was wealthy?

She felt sick as Matt confirmed it. 'He sent me a letter saying he wanted to see me. I put it in the bin. But then he turned up on the doorstep. Thankfully Mum was out at physio. No way was I letting him in the house, in case I couldn't get rid of him—I didn't want her to have to face him. So I went with him to the park. I sat on a bench with him and listened to what he had to say. He told me the garage wasn't doing so well, he was having a hard time making the loan payments, and he thought I might like to help my poor old dad out a bit.'

'Did you?'

Matt closed his eyes. 'I reminded him that he'd walked out on all of us five years before, he'd not remembered a single one of our birthdays, and he hadn't paid my mum a penny since he left—we'd spent years struggling for money with Lucy, Annie and I all having a part-time job while we were at school, to help pay the bills. So, yes, I quite understood what it was like to have financial problems. And I was sure he'd quite understand that, as he hadn't wanted to know us for the last five years, none of us wanted to know him now. Then I walked away and I haven't heard from him since.' He gave her a wry smile. 'I kind of feel a bit guilty because I had the money. I could've helped him out, and it's not nice to see people struggle. But I can't forgive him for how he treated my mum and my sisters.'

She noted that he didn't say anything about the way his father had treated him—walking out on him, leaving him to support the family at the age of fifteen, and then only getting in touch when he thought Matt was rich. It must've hurt. Yet Matt still put his mum and his sisters first. Responsibility and duty were clearly a very strong part of who he was.

'For what it's worth,' she said, 'I don't think you owed him anything.'

'I didn't like how it made me feel—as if I was

stooping to his level. If he'd sent a birthday card to the girls, or picked up the phone to wish them happy birthday... Then I might've felt differently. If I thought he'd cared about them, I would've helped him.'

'But he didn't care about anyone except himself. I think if my dad had done something like that to us,' she said, 'Posy would've cut up all his shirts, Portia would've drop-kicked him into the middle of next week, and Andie and I would've strapped him to the wing of a plane and done some seriously nasty acrobatics.'

'Never upset the Marlowe girls, hmm?' Matt asked wryly.

'Absolutely. Portia was all ready to come home and scalp Stephen when I told her why the wedding was off, and Andie would've done the same if she hadn't still been having a bit of morning sickness. And when Javier...' She stopped.

'Javier?' he prompted.

'Let's just say there was a point where I was going to get on a plane and straighten him out about who my sister really is and what she would never, ever do. And he might have crawled to her on his knees and begged her forgiveness by the time I'd finished. Though thankfully it didn't come to that.'

'I think,' he said, 'I'll make sure I keep on the right side of the Marlowe sisters.'

She smiled. 'I don't think you'll have any problems. Andie thinks you're a sweetheart, Portia likes you, and although you haven't really met Posy properly I'm pretty sure she'll like you, too.'

He inclined his head. 'Thank you, but I wasn't fishing for compliments.'

'You weren't getting any. It's a statement of fact,' she said. 'You're one of the good guys, Matt.'

'Well, thank you anyway.' He shrugged. 'I'm just me.'

And, the more Immi got to know him, the more she liked him. The more she respected him.

She had a nasty feeling that it would be very easy to fall in love with Matt Stark.

To distract both of them, she said, 'I managed to get in touch with the flying club. They're going to rent me a plane on Thursday morning, if you'd like to come.'

'Sounds good. What time?'

'I'll pick you up in Sofia's car at ten,' she said.

'You're sure the old car's up to it?'

'You're good with computers, right, so you could fix something that stopped working?' she asked.

'Yes.'

'That would be me with engines, so if the car conks out on us I can get it going again.' Too late, she remembered that his father was a mechanic, and wished the words unsaid.

It must've shown in her expression, because he stooped to kiss her. 'Not all mechanics are lying, cheating cowards.'

'I'm sorry for—'

'Don't apologise,' he cut in, and kissed her again. 'Let's forget about him and go have dinner.'

'Yeah.'

Their lovemaking that night felt even more tender; Matt had opened up to her about his past, and it had drawn them closer. Though Immi was horribly aware she still hadn't told him the truth about herself. But this was three weeks out of time. A summer fling to help each other out of the place where they were stuck. It didn't mean they were going to fall in love and be together for ever... Did it?

CHAPTER EIGHT

ON THURSDAY, IMMI called in to bring Gloria more flowers before she collected Matt.

'Are you ready for this?' she asked with a grin.

'I think so.'

'I've booked us a four-seater. It's about the size of a Marlowe Nymph,' she said, 'so it's pretty much what I'm used to flying.'

Matt hadn't really seen Immi animated like this before. Flying was clearly what lit her up from the inside—the way he felt when he was studying the stars. It was a new side to her, and one he rather liked. 'I'm looking forward to it. Is it a pain if I bring my camera?'

'Definitely bring it,' she said, 'because you'll get some amazing shots. Before we leave, I'd better ask if you get travel-sick—in which case I'd say take the tablets right now.'

'It's fine. I don't get travel-sick.'

'Good, but if you've not flown in a small plane before you might find it a bit different from what you've done before. The weather's pretty much perfect today, but we still might get caught off guard by an air current. There'll be a sick bag in the knee board if you need it.'

'Knee board?' he asked.

'The plane equivalent of a glove box in a car,' she said with a smile.

'Bring it on,' he said, smiling back.

Once at the airfield, he climbed into the plane. There wasn't quite as much room as he'd been expecting; she hadn't been joking about the plane being small. But, sitting next to her, he could see the control panel of the plane—and it was fascinating.

Immi glanced at him. 'OK?'

'More than OK.' He grinned at her. 'This is going to be great. I've never done anything like this before.'

'I probably ought to warn you that this is like

driving in an older car instead of a modern with good suspension—you're going to feel all the bumps and it's a little bit spartan.'

'Like Sofia's ancient car?' he teased.

She grinned back. 'Yes. And it's way more fun than driving a modern car because you have to think about what you're doing. Nothing beats it.' She handed him a set of headphones with a microphone. 'Use this to talk to me during the flight,' she said, 'otherwise you won't hear a word over the noise of the plane.'

'Thanks.' He paused. 'Is it OK to sling the camera round my neck?'

'Absolutely.'

He couldn't resist taking a shot of her as she ran through the pre-flight checks; she was serious, intense and focused, yet at the same time she seemed lit up from the inside. This was clearly what she loved most.

She started the plane and taxied to the runway. He could see the rotor blades whirring in front of the window, and he could feel the adrenalin running through his veins, the edge of anticipation he always felt before take-off—except this time he wasn't sitting in a comfortable seat, oblivious to what the pilot was doing. This was up close and personal.

'We're taking off now,' she said.

Just as she'd warned him, he could feel the little bumps in the runway and hear the thrum of the tyres—then there was less of a sound and suddenly they were in the air. It was so smooth that it took him by surprise. 'We're flying!'

'Yup.' He could hear the smile in her voice. 'Look down at the ground. You'll see the shadow of the plane as we turn.'

'That's amazing. I can see *us*.' He took a few shots with his camera, making sure to get the plane's shadow in the frame.

He'd flown quite a few times before, but it had been nothing like this. The views from the cockpit were spectacular, from the sun shimmering on the sea through to the mountainous, forested centre of the island. It was a totally different perspective, and he loved it.

'I can see now how the island got its name,' he said. 'I had no idea there was so much bougainvillea, and that it came in so many different colours. Or that the sea around the island would have so many different shades of blue.'

'Usually the turquoise bits in the sea are shallow and the darker blue shows deeper water. I'd love to fly over the Atlantic and watch the whales,' she said, sounding wistful. 'It must be incredible to see a pod below you like that.'

'I'm putting that on my bucket list,' he said. 'I love this, Immi. I wasn't expecting it to be anything like this. I've only ever flown in commercial aircraft before—jets where you can hear the engine whining and you feel pushed back into your seat on takeoff. This is so different.'

He could see from her expression that she was pleased he understood why she loved it. 'This is a borrowed plane so I can't let you take the controls,' she said. 'But if you ever come over to

Cambridge, I'll take you up in a Marlowe plane and you can fly it when we're airborne.'

Something about the idea snagged his attention. 'Have you ever taught anyone to fly?'

'No.'

'Maybe,' he said, 'that's something you could think about. A way out of your crossroads.'

'I don't think Dad would want to set up a flying school division,' she said.

'Just an idea,' he said lightly.

'And it's appreciated. I'll think about it.'

He backed off and let her talk to him about flying. And then she said casually, 'Recognise where we are?'

He looked down to see the national park around the village. 'That's Baio di Rosa,' he said. 'And the villa. Neptune's Arch.'

'You should be over your house about…ooh… now.'

He took a barrage of shots, knowing that his mother and sisters would love them.

And then, all too soon, their hour was up and Immi landed the plane. What was it Cleve had

said? He'd fallen in love with Andie the day he'd
seen her land a plane, light as a feather. Matt had
a nasty feeling that it would be all too easy for
him to fall in love with Andie's twin. He liked
the neat, precise way she did things. The joy she
found in flying. And, when she looked at him
after the plane had stopped, her hazel eyes had
turned the purest gold.

'That,' he said when he'd climbed out of the
plane, 'was amazing.'

'Yeah. I love flying.'

She'd shared her big love with him. And now
he wanted to do the same with her. 'Weather per-
mitting, how do you fancy doing some proper
stargazing on Saturday night?'

'What we did the other night, when you taught
me the constellations?'

'Close up,' he said.

'There's an observatory on L'Isola dei Fiori?'

'No. We'll use the same spot,' he said. 'With
my telescope.'

'I'd love that.' She reached up and kissed him.
'Bring it on.'

* * *

After Matt had left her that evening, Immi grew thoughtful.

Teaching.

She'd never considered the possibility before; she'd always been focused on working for Marlowe Aviation. Paying back the love and care her parents had given her—and, if she was honest, keeping a safety net for herself.

But maybe teaching others to fly was a possibility. Just out of sheer curiosity, she looked up flight instruction on the internet. There was a six-week course at the local flying school that would teach her how to teach, prepare and give lectures, and do pre-flight briefings. She already had her pilot's licence and met all the course's pre-entry conditions of flying experience, so there was no reason why she couldn't take the course.

Could this be her way out of the crossroads?

It would be a job where she could be with planes all the time, rather than having to retrain and do something that didn't have such a hold on her heart. And, if she taught part-time, she could still do the testing at Marlowe Aviation; someone else could fill in her role on the admin side and put up with Stephen.

She'd need to talk it over with her family, first. But maybe this was her way forward—thanks to Matt.

On Saturday evening, Matt brought his telescope over and set it up by their bench overlooking the sea. 'The moon is perfect tonight,' he said. 'It's the first quarter, so you can see everything at an angle.' He checked through the eyepiece, then beckoned to her. 'Come and have a look.'

She bent her head to look through the eyepiece. 'Matt, this is amazing—like the pictures you see on the internet. I can't believe how much detail there is.'

'Craters and seas and mountains.' He rested one hand on her shoulder and talked her through what she was seeing.

'So can you see the other planets like you can see the moon?'

'Not quite,' he said. 'I can show you Venus.'

She stepped aside to let him adjust the telescope.

'You won't get any fine detail like you do with the moon,' he warned, 'because the planet's surface is enveloped in thick mist, but you'll see its phase.'

Just as he'd said, when she looked through the eyepiece the planet looked like a white disc. 'I take it Venus is full right now?' she asked, disappointed.

'Yes.'

'So if you can't see any detail, you wouldn't be able to see Saturn's rings?'

He smiled. 'Saturn's not visible right now, but I can show you pictures I've taken through the telescope from here—and the rings are definitely visible.'

'Uh-huh.'

'Jupiter's a bit more interesting.' He adjusted the telescope again. 'Try this.'

'Oh—there's the red spot!' she said, surprised. 'And it's stripy. I wasn't expecting that.'

'Cloud bands. And you should be able to see the four Galilean moons.'

'The colours keep changing,' she said, surprised.

'Atmospherics,' he explained.

'The reason why stars twinkle, right?'

'Right.' He stole a kiss. 'Do you remember me showing you Cassiopeia?'

She nodded. 'The W-shaped constellation.'

'Let me show you a close-up.' He adjusted the telescope again. 'What do you see?'

'Two very bright stars,' she said promptly.

'Look a bit harder around it. If I tell you it's called the Owl Cluster...'

'The bright stars are the eyes, right?'

'Right.'

'And I can just about make out the shape of an owl's outstretched wings. I totally get why the stars fascinate you,' she said. 'This is amazing.'

'Like you and your planes.'

238 THE RUNAWAY BRIDE AND THE BILLIONAIRE

She straightened up. 'Thanks to you, I've got a pretty good idea of what I'm going to do. I'm going to talk to Dad when I get back to England, and either set up a flying school division for Marlowe's, or work part-time at another school and still do the testing for Marlowe's. So then it doesn't matter if Stephen stays—I won't have to deal with him.'

'That's good.' He kissed her.

'Are you any nearer to deciding what you want to do?'

'Apart from the travelling, no. I'm planning to start with Mauna Kea in Hawaii—it's open to the public and there's a solar telescope as well.'

'That sounds good.'

'Yeah. And I wouldn't have gone if you hadn't made me think a bit harder. So you've really helped me with this crossroads thing, too.'

'I'm glad.'

Yet, at the same time, she was sad. It was so ironic that Matt Stark was everything she wanted in a partner: he was kind, clever, and being with him made the world seem a much better place. But, in a couple of weeks' time, she'd be going back to England. Matt's life, when he came back from travelling, would be here on the island. If they wanted to stay together, one or other of them would have to make a huge compromise—such a huge change in their lives that there was a real risk they'd start to resent each other.

She just had to remind herself that this was temporary.

Matt and Immi still hadn't managed to snatch a night together where they could wake up in each other's arms, but they managed to see each other every day.

They were sitting looking out to sea one night on the bench in the arbour, and Immi was picking out the constellations Matt had taught her.

'You're getting good at this,' he said.

'I had a good teacher,' she said. 'I imagine you did this with your sisters?'

'I did, and I'll do the same with my nieces and

nephews.' He paused. 'Though I once thought I'd do this with my own children.'

And Matt Stark would be way more of a father than his own had ever been.

Then it hit her what he'd just said, and she went cold. 'You do want children still, then?' she asked.

He grimaced. 'In a way, I've already been there and done that, helping to bring up my sisters.'

'And you don't want to do it all over again?'

'No,' he said. 'Which probably makes me selfish.'

She smiled. 'You're the least selfish man I've ever met—and, trust me, I've met a few in my time.' And the fact that he didn't want children also gave her hope. If he wanted this thing between them to keep going, then her past might not be such a huge barrier.

'How about you?' he asked. 'Do you want children?'

Yes. No. Maybe.

She could make an anodyne response. Or she

could be honest with him. She had nothing to lose—and potentially a whole world to gain.

'It's a bit more complicated than that for me,' she said. 'You know I told you I had a few body issues when I was a teenager?'

He nodded.

'I had anorexia,' she said. 'It probably started in my early teens when I overheard my grand-parents talking about me, and it was all "Well, she's not like Andie"—I was never quite good enough. Andie was the slim, pretty, clever twin, and I wasn't.'

He frowned. 'I like Andie enormously—but in no way do you not match up to her, Immi.'

'I didn't in some areas,' Immi said, wanting to be truthful. 'She's amazing at maths and physics. I could never quite match her grades—and one of my teachers actually said that at parents' evening.'

'In front of you?' He looked shocked.

'In front of both of us. Andie was furious and had a go at the teacher for being rude, and pointed out that I was better in other subjects than she was but those teachers would never be so unprofessional as to say it in front of us.' She smiled. 'Andie's always had my back, just as I always had hers.'

'Did she hear what your grandparents said?'

'No, and I didn't tell her, or she and Portia would've hung them out to dry. It's not their fault,' she said swiftly. 'It's me being stupid and adolescent and letting other people make me feel inadequate.' She grimaced. 'I comfort ate for a bit. And then this boy at school asked me out. He was the coolest boy in school. I couldn't believe that Shaun actually wanted to date me. I was so thrilled.'

He had a nasty feeling he knew where this was going, and he held her closer.

'I gave him my virginity,' she said. 'He made me feel so special. Until...' She dragged in a breath. 'We were at a party. I wasn't feeling very well and I couldn't find him, so I went to get my coat. And there he was, on the bed, under all the coats, having sex with another girl.'

Immi clearly wasn't very good at picking Mr Right, he thought. Her first serious boyfriend had been a cheater. So had her fiancé.

'And he laughed at me,' she said. 'He asked me why I thought anyone would ever want to date Immi the Elephant, the fattest girl in sixth form. He'd only dated me for a bet.' She dragged in a breath. 'He'd slept with me for a bet. Not because he liked me.'

Matt felt his fists clench. 'It wasn't you,' he said. 'Shaun sounds very immature and very, very stupid.'

'I didn't even know people called me Immi the Elephant,' she said. 'I was horrified to realise that everyone in the sixth form was laughing at me. So I dieted. And when the weight wouldn't come off fast enough, I went running. And when that didn't work, I took laxatives and I bought diet pills off the internet. I was so desperate to be beautiful.'

'Oh, Immi.' His heart ached for her. Couldn't she see how beautiful she was?

'I hid it from everyone at home. I wore baggy jumpers and baggy jeans so nobody could see my shape. But I wanted to be thin. I so wanted to be thin.' She dragged in a breath. 'Eventually Andie twigged what was happening, and she made me talk to Mum. They made me go to the doctor, and he was shocked at how much weight I'd lost. He suggested counselling.' She looked away. 'Which is how come I took my A levels a year after my twin. Andie aced her exams and got her pilot's licence, and I was meant to do it at the same time—but I didn't get my grades. I had to resit the year; and I spent a lot of time that year having counselling.'

'Did the counselling work?' he asked gently.

'Yes.' She sighed. 'But my mum and my sisters all blame themselves for not noticing that I was starving myself in front of them. They hug me every time they see me, and it's not just because they love me—they're checking how I feel, to see if I've lost any weight and if they need to step in. They look at my collarbones before they look at my face. They can't get past the fear that I'll do it again. And that's why I've been taking pictures of my food, sending them to my mum and my sisters—so they know I'm definitely eating and I'm not slipping back into...' She wrinkled her nose. 'Illness, I guess.'

'Oh, Immi. I'm sorry you had to go through that.'

'It's not just the eating,' she said. 'The counselling sorted me out and I'm able to deal with things a lot better than I used to. I don't feel inadequate any more. But although it's a mental illness, it has physical consequences. My periods stopped for a while, and there's a good chance I might not be able to have children, even if I have IVF treatment.'

'I'm sorry,' he said. 'There's a world of difference between not wanting children and having your choices taken away.'

'I've come to terms with it. Stephen said he

didn't want children, so it wasn't an issue for him,' she said. 'But for all I know he was lying about that, too. Maybe that's one of the reasons he cheated on me.'

'Or maybe he was just an unprincipled bastard. Which is his problem, not yours,' Matt said. 'You know what I said about violence not solving anything?'

She nodded.

'I really want to punch Shaun the Stupid and Stephen the Scumbag.'

'You'll have to join the queue behind my sisters—and me,' Immi said. 'Portia says that if I date anyone else whose first name begins with S, she'll kidnap me until I come to my senses.'

He grinned. 'I like Portia. Even if she *is* scary.'

'Anyway. So now you know the whole truth about me.'

He kissed her. 'I can assure you it won't go any further than me. And thank you for trusting me.' He paused. 'Are you OK about Andie and Cleve?'

'And the baby? More than OK. I might never be a mum,' she said, 'but I can be the best aunt in the world. Well, joint best aunt,' she amended. 'Portia and Posy will be just as great.'

'Yeah.' He stroked her face. 'What you've just told me—it doesn't make any difference to you and me.'

Because this thing between them had a time limit?

Or because he really didn't want children and thought they could share other things together?

She wasn't sure which; but, when he leaned over and kissed her, she kissed him back to the point where they ended up making love underneath the stars, to the sound of the waves on the shore below. And there was something sweeter and more tender about the way he touched her, almost as if he was scared that she'd break.

But she wasn't going to break. She'd worked too hard to become stronger and overcome all her self-doubts.

CHAPTER NINE

ON THE MONDAY of her last week at the villa, Immi woke feeling odd, with a strange metallic taste in her mouth.

A metallic taste.

Wasn't that what Andie had told her she'd experienced when she'd fallen pregnant?

Immi sucked in a deep breath. No way. No way could she be pregnant. From what she'd read about the physical effects of her illness, she'd need IVF treatment and a lot of luck.

All the same, she counted back in her head. Her period should have started a day or two ago. She hadn't really been thinking about it, and with all the emotional upset over the past couple of months it wouldn't be surprising if her cycle had gone a bit awry. Of course she wasn't pregnant.

But the idea wouldn't leave her head.

And she couldn't settle to anything. Work in the garden did nothing to soothe her worries, and neither did listening to music.

Then her phone beeped with a text. It was Andie's twin-sense kicking in again, Immi thought wryly as she looked at the screen.

Are you OK? Just had this feeling...

No, she wasn't OK. She was all over the place. She'd thought for years that she would probably never have children and she'd told herself that she was fine with just being an aunt. Now there was the possibility that she might be having a baby of her own... And, if that was the case, what next?

I'm fine, nothing to worry about at all, she lied.

But panic flooded through her. Matt was the one she ought to be talking to about this. But how could she, when she knew he had such a strong sense of duty and responsibility—one that had been heightened by seeing how far his father had fallen short of fulfilling his responsibilities? She was pretty sure that Matt's immediate response would be to cancel his plans to go travelling. He'd stand by her, because he'd see it as his duty to be there for the baby.

And that wasn't fair to him.

Matt had never resented his mother and his sisters for a second, but instead of being a normal teen he'd been a carer and a father figure. He'd turned down a place to study the subject that made him light up from the inside, so he could make sure that his family was looked after properly. Now he finally had the chance to do something for himself, and he'd decided to travel, giving himself enough space and time to work out what he really wanted to do with his future. He'd planned to start by visiting a telescopic array in Hawaii he'd only ever read about. Something he'd never had the chance to see.

How could she take that away from him? He'd be trapped. Even though he'd told her he didn't want children, he'd cancel all his plans and give up his future for the baby without a second thought for himself, she knew. And it really wasn't fair to him. Or to her—she didn't want him to be with her out of duty. She wanted him to be with her because he *wanted* to be there.

And, although he'd been really understanding about her past, her old anxieties resurfaced. He'd said he didn't want any commitments, but she knew he'd stand by her because he believed in duty and responsibility. All the time she'd find herself wondering if she was really enough for him.

What was she going to do?

Her first instinct was to call one of her sisters. But Andie and Portia were newlyweds and she didn't want to dump all her problems on them, and Posy had gone elusive. Her mother would cry and her father would rant and rave. Her friends from university and work knew nothing about her struggles with anorexia in her teens, and she wanted to keep it that way—the last thing she wanted was for yet more people to worry about her and watch her collarbones. She wanted people to see her as she was now, and not see her through the lens of her past illness.

So it looked as if she was going to have to deal with this on her own.

L'Isola dei Fiori wasn't the place for her to do that. She didn't want to buy a pregnancy test in the village and have everyone asking questions—or, worse still, saying something to Matt before she could talk to him. OK, so she could drive all the way out to San Rocco to find an anonymous supermarket; but all she really wanted to do right now was to go home. In Cambridge, she'd be in familiar surroundings: home, where she was used to dealing with things and organising things.

It was a plan. One that worked for her. She'd go home, buy a pregnancy test and then find out if the unthinkable really had happened.

And then she'd cope with the results.

It didn't take long to book a taxi, a ferry crossing and her flight home to England. Once she'd packed, she planned to call Matt from the ferry to say goodbye and wish him luck in his travels. They could part as friends. And she'd deal with the fallout of the situation once she was back home.

It was a risk, Matt thought. He'd told Immi that he didn't want any commitments, and she'd said the same. They'd agreed to spend three weeks together, simply helping each other over a crossroads. And now those three weeks were almost up.

Except his heart hadn't been listening to the 'no commitments' bit.

Over those few days, he'd fallen in love with her. He'd fallen in love with a strong, bright woman who'd had to work hard to overcome the problems of her teenage years—but she'd definitely overcome them enough to talk to him about them and trust him with her confidence. Which made him pretty sure that she felt the same closeness that he did, because Immi wasn't the sort to wear her heart on her sleeve and tell everyone what she was feeling every second of the day. Confiding in him had meant something to her.

He knew she shared his sense of adventure, and she'd helped him to think about a compromise so he could follow his heart without feeling that he was letting his mother down or dumping his responsibilities. She was the first woman he'd ever met that he could actually imagine sharing his life with—someone who'd take the rough with the smooth, who'd come up with solutions instead of just moaning about a problem, who'd be there for him as well as expecting him to be there for her.

So now was the time to tell her how he felt. To ask her to go travelling with him and then make a future with him.

She wasn't in the garden, where he'd half expected to find her. He knocked on the back door; there was no answer. Frowning, he tried the door, and it opened.

'Immi?' he called, stepping into the hallway.

'Oh—Matt!' She came out of the bedroom, looking flustered. 'I wasn't expecting to see you.'

'Is everything all right?' he asked.

'Yes. I, um—I'm going back to England.'

He frowned. 'I thought you weren't going back for another few days yet?'

She shrugged. 'Well, I've made my mind up about what I want to do, so I think it's time to go back home and sort out the rest of my life.'

He couldn't quite believe this. 'So you're leaving right now?'

'I'm just finishing packing. The taxi will be here in half an hour.'

He stared at her, hardly able to process what she was saying. *I wasn't expecting to see you... I'm just finishing packing...* 'You were going to leave without even saying goodbye to me?'

'I…um…' She looked uncomfortable, and Matt's heart sank. So much for thinking that they could have a future together. She clearly hadn't changed her stance of not wanting a commitment—and now it was pretty obvious that she wanted a clean break. To go home and start her new life. Without him.

She didn't share his feelings.

It was just as well that he hadn't made an idiot of himself by telling her how he felt. And he wasn't going to make her feel guilty about the fact she didn't feel the same way about him. She'd been honest with him—well, up until now.

What was the saying about loving someone enough to let them go? Because he didn't want to hold her back. Even though it really hurt that she'd planned to leave without a word.

'Since you've booked a taxi, I guess you don't need a lift to the ferry,' he said.

'I'm sorry.' She stared at the floor. 'But we said no commitments. And you're going travelling in a few days. So I guess…'

He didn't want to end things on such a sour note, so he'd make this easy for her. 'Well, good luck with the training course. I'm sure you'll make an excellent flying instructor.'

'Thanks. And good luck with the travelling. I hope you get to see some really amazing places.'

'Thanks.' What now? Should he make some anodyne remark about staying in touch? He probably ought to, but he couldn't face it. *'Arrivederci,'* he said.

She nodded. 'Um—maybe you could say goodbye to your mum for me?'

'Sure,' Matt said, keeping his voice as level and expressionless as he could. 'Safe journey home.'

'Thank you. For everything.'

Thankfully she didn't hug him or try to kiss his cheek. He couldn't have handled that. He simply gave her a cool nod and backed away.

Leaving the villa was a blur. Matt didn't want to go straight home, either, because his mother knew him well enough to notice that something was wrong. The last thing he felt like doing was talking about what a fool he'd nearly made of himself—how he'd been stupid enough to fall for someone who didn't feel the same way. So instead he drove to the next village—the one where he'd taken Immi to dinner at the restaurant overlooking the sea. The night they'd made love. The night she'd opened up to him about her past. It felt like a lifetime away.

He'd still go travelling. He'd still visit the solar telescope in Hawaii and discover new places.

Just it would be without her.

The taxi was on time, as was the ferry and then the flight. And all the way home Immi felt guilty. She'd seen the hurt on Matt's face when he'd thought she'd planned to leave without even saying goodbye; she hated the fact that she'd made him feel bad, but what else could she have done? If she'd told him about her suspicions, he would've cancelled his trip. She didn't want to take away his chance of doing something to please himself for the first time in years and years and years.

Once she'd gone through passport control and customs, she picked up a pregnancy test at the pharmacy in the airport, then called into the small supermarket for bread and milk and a meal she could shove in the microwave when she got home. She ordered a taxi to take her back from the airport to her flat. Again, she felt guilty, because she hadn't even told her family that she was coming home; but she needed to get things straight in her head before she talked to anyone—even her twin.

Back at her flat, she opened all the windows to air the place, which smelled dusty and stale. She unpacked, put everything away and started doing the laundry; and then she'd run out of excuses and she couldn't avoid the situation any longer.

She took a deep breath, and headed for the bathroom. In two minutes' time, she'd know exactly what she was dealing with. A false alarm— or a life-changing event.

She'd never taken a pregnancy test, but she knew from Andie and from friends what to expect. Pee on the stick, wait for a couple of minutes, and then check for a little blue line.

What she hadn't expected was for time to slow

down. Since when did a second take so long? For a moment she wondered if her watch had actually stopped working. But no: it was just taking several heartbeats for a second to pass. Or maybe her heart rate had speeded up to rocket propulsion levels.

One blue line to show that the test was working. So that was one less thing to worry about.

She waited, watching the test stick closely. Staring at it as if her life depended on it—and in some ways it did. Waiting. Waiting.

Two minutes *had* to be up by now. And still there wasn't a second blue line.

She glanced at her watch. Two and a half minutes.

So there it was. The truth. She wasn't pregnant; clearly her cycle had been thrown by the stress of the last couple of months.

She knew she ought to feel relieved. She wasn't in a mess and didn't have to turn anyone else's life upside down with unexpected news. It was a good thing that she wasn't pregnant and alone.

But part of her wished she hadn't been such a coward and rushed straight back home. That she'd taken the test in L'Isola dei Fiori instead, and spent those last few precious days with Matt…

'Don't be so ridiculous, Imogen Marlowe,' she told herself fiercely. 'A couple of days wouldn't have made any difference.' It would just have been a couple more days where she would've fallen that bit more deeply in love with Matt— which would've been foolish, given that they'd both agreed it was a fling to help them over a crossroads, and then they'd walk out of each other's lives.

No commitments. They'd both been clear on that. They'd had almost three weeks together and they'd both planned to move on.

She stared at the test stick again. She'd thought she'd come to terms with the fact that children probably weren't going to be part of her future— but right now all she felt was empty. And very, very alone.

She wasn't quite ready to face her family yet; she wanted to be a little bit more together, first, so nobody would guess that anything might be wrong and then rush straight into overprotective mode. Although she planned to have a long bath and then an early night, she found herself lying awake, wondering what Matt was doing. Which was stupid, because she'd definitely burned her bridges as far as he was concerned. And who was to say she'd even done the right thing? She'd thought she was being so noble and unselfish, giving him the chance to travel and find out what he really wanted from life. But instead had she been arrogant and selfish, making a decision for him when she really didn't have the right to do that?

In the end, she decided it would be better to do something more useful than lying there fretting, so she got up and made a list of what she needed to do tomorrow: speak to her father about a change in her role at Marlowe Aviation, call the flying school to book a place on the course, arrange appointments with a couple of estate agents to see which one she wanted to sell her flat, and then spring-clean the flat so it was ready to be put on the market.

There was an item she didn't write down but it was at the top of the list anyway.

Miss Matt.

And she had a feeling it was going to be like that for a long, long time.

CHAPTER TEN

MATT WALKED INTO the airport. He'd already said
his goodbyes to his mother, but this felt strange.
When he'd first booked his trip to Hawaii, he'd
pretty much assumed that Immi would wave him
off from the airport before she went back to England herself.

But Immi had already left. She'd wished him
good luck and safe travels. And Matt didn't feel
the slightest bit excited about his plans to travel
the world and see a solar telescope. He just felt
alone.

He checked in, then went to the café to grab
an espresso.

Something was nagging in the back of his head.

Immi had gone back to England early. She
hadn't even given him a real reason for her

change of plan. And the Immi he'd come to know, the Immi who'd confided in him about her difficult past, wasn't the kind of woman to leave without saying goodbye.

He'd missed something. But what?

He thought about it as his gate opened.

He thought about it a bit more as the 'now boarding' sign flashed up on the announcements board.

He thought about it a bit more as the 'last call' announcement came across on the Tannoy.

She'd been badly let down by her first boyfriend and by her ex-fiancé. What if she'd gone home early because she thought Matt still wanted no commitments, and she needed to be the one to leave first, this time? OK, so she'd said 'no commitments', too. But feelings changed. They'd grown close. And maybe instead of trying to be selfless and letting her go, he should've been honest with her and told her how he felt.

Though it wasn't too late to do that. He could change his plans. Instead of going to Hawaii, he could do what he should've done yesterday—talk to Immi. Properly. Because right now he had nothing to lose: if she didn't feel the same way about him, then he'd still be where he was now. But if she did share his feelings, not saying anything could lose him the love of a lifetime.

He wasn't prepared to do that. He'd take the risk of opening his heart and telling her how he felt.

Luckily he'd decided to travel super-light with only carry-on luggage, so he didn't have to worry about causing problems for the airline. He picked up his case, headed for the desk and rebooked his flight—for a different destination.

Immi was in the middle of scrubbing the flat clean when she heard a knock on her door.

Odd. She wasn't expecting anyone. Besides, the postman or a visitor would've rung the intercom in the lobby. It was probably one of the neighbours who'd heard a noise, thought she was still away, and was checking that every-thing was OK.

She answered the door and stared in surprise. 'Matt! What are you...? Aren't you supposed to be packing for your trip to Hawaii?'

'I changed my plans,' he said. 'Can I come in? Because I'd really rather not have this conversa-tion on your doorstep.'

'But how did you...?'

'Know where you live? I asked Andie,' he said. 'And one of your neighbours let me in.'

'I—um—do you want some coffee?'

'No, I just want to talk to you.'

'OK.' She stood aside to let him in and re-moved her rubber gloves. 'Sorry, it's a bit of a mess because I wasn't expecting visitors.'

'You're doing a bit of spring-cleaning?'

'I'm getting the flat ready to sell,' she admitted.

'So you can buy a house with a garden?'

He actually remembered her telling him that? She nodded.

'How would you feel,' he asked, 'about a house with a garden and a granny annexe?'

'A granny annexe?' Her heart skipped a beat. That was something else she'd said to him, about his own situation. Was he suggesting…?

'When I came to see you yesterday,' he said, 'I did something very stupid.'

Not knowing what to say, she waited for him to elaborate.

'I let you walk away without telling you how I feel,' he said. 'I thought I was being noble and selfless in letting you go to your new life. And it's the biggest mistake I've ever made.' He drew a deep breath. 'I know we both said no commitments, but that's not what I want any more. I want *you*, Immi. By my side. For the rest of our lives.'

He wanted her? She couldn't quite process that. 'But you're going travelling.'

'I planned to ask you to come with me. But then I came in and you were packing, and I thought maybe you didn't feel the same way about me that I feel about you.'

'The way you feel about me?'

'I fell in love with you, Immi. With a woman who loves walking at the edge of the sea, who adores pottering around in the garden, and who literally reaches for the sky. With a woman who's shown me things from a new perspective—I look at the world in a different way since I met you. And I want to be with you.' He took a deep breath. 'So that's why I'm here, because I want to spend the rest of my life with you.'

She looked at him as if she didn't quite believe him.

'I know you've been let down,' he said softly. 'Shaun and Stephen both used you. But I don't see you as a woman I could use to win a bet or further my career. I see you for who you are, Immi. A strong, clever, capable woman. One who'd fight for what she believes in, and who'd take apart anyone who upset any of her sisters. I see a woman who's cool and calm enough to handle flying a tiny plane. A woman with the most beautiful hazel eyes, which go green when she's sad and gold when she's happy or...' He couldn't resist rubbing the pad of his thumb along her lower lip. 'When she climaxes,' he whispered, and was gratified to see colour blooming in her cheeks.

'I see a woman who's kind and generous enough to do things for other people when her own life's in total upheaval—visiting my mum, sorting out your sister's garden. A woman who's holding back from doing something she really wants in her career, putting herself second, because she doesn't want to let her family down.'

'That,' she said, 'is definitely a case of pots and kettles.'

'Not quite,' he said, 'because right now I'm putting myself first and I'm fighting for what I really want. I might not be making as good a job of it as I'd like to, but hear me out. I see a woman whose smile makes me feel as if the whole night sky has just lit up. A woman who feels like the perfect fit in my arms. A woman who makes me believe I can do anything because she's by my side. The most beautiful woman in the world.' He paused. 'I see *you*, Imogen Marlowe. The woman I want to spend the rest of my life with—if you'll have me. Will you marry me?'

She hadn't told him about her pregnancy scare—but he was here anyway. Not out of a sense of duty and responsibility, but because he really, really loved her.

She'd been let down before. But Matthew Stark wasn't the kind of man who let people down. He was a good, decent, honest man. Someone she could rely on. And more. 'I love you, too,' she whispered. 'But we said no commitments.'

'Is that why you walked away?'

'It's comp—'

'—licated,' he finished, and stroked her cheek.

She gave him a rueful smile. 'Yeah. But I owe you the truth, Matt. I wasn't completely honest with you.' She swallowed hard. 'I didn't leave the island because I wanted to start my new life and couldn't wait. I walked away because I wanted you to have the chance to do the things you really wanted to do.'

He frowned. 'I don't understand.'

'If I'd told you why I was really coming home, you would have come with me. You would have given up your travels.'

'Which I just did—at least, I've put them on hold because I want to share them with you,' he said.

She shook her head. 'I mean you would have seen me as your duty. Your responsibility.'

'Why?'

'Because I thought I was pregnant.'

His eyes went wide. 'But I thought you said you couldn't…?'

'I'm not pregnant,' she said. 'Probably all the stress of the last couple of months made me miss a period. I did a test when I came home.'

'And you weren't going to tell me?'

'I would have told you when you were back

from your travels,' she said. 'I knew I probably should have told you when I realised I was late. I should have done a test on the island. But I panicked. You told me you didn't want children. And I needed some space to work out what to do. OK, the test was negative, but what if it had been positive?'

'I...' He raked his hand through his hair. 'I didn't want children. But I would have stood by you.'

'I know. And I didn't want you to have to give up your dreams again. I didn't want to be a burden.'

He gave her a rueful smile. 'So basically we were both trying to be noble. You were trying to let me go to see all the places I'd never been able to visit, and I was going to let you go because I didn't want to make you feel bad about not having the same feelings for me that I did about you.' He raised an eyebrow. 'I think being noble might be overrated.'

'So you're not angry with me? For not telling you?'

'No,' he said. 'I came after you today for *you*, Immi. I didn't know about the baby.'

'The baby that isn't,' she reminded him. 'I still might not be able to have children. What if you change your mind and decide that you do want kids?'

'Then we have options. Just the same as if you decide that you really want to have children. So the doctors told you there might be a problem?'

'They didn't tell me specifically. I read a few articles,' she admitted.

'Then our first step would be to talk to the doctors, and have tests,' he said. 'If it means IVF, then we try IVF. And if that doesn't work, we could foster or adopt. Or we can just enjoy being an aunt and uncle—between us we have one and a bit nieces and nephews already, and with seven sisters between us I reckon we have a good chance of having a few more.'

She dragged in a breath. 'But even if we put

the issue of children aside, we live in different places. You live on the island with your mum, and I live here in England.'

'Then we'll find a compromise,' he said. 'We'll talk it through. If you want to live in Cambridge and Mum wants to stay on the island, Cambridge is at least near an international airport. A three-hour flight and an hour on the ferry—that's as long as it would take us to drive from Cambridge to the Lake District, if Mum was still living in our old family home in England.' He paused. 'Or Mum might even consider coming back to England, at least for the summer months. That way she'd get to see a lot more of the girls. Especially now she's a grandmother.'

'That big house with a granny annexe,' she said thoughtfully. 'We could do that in Cambridge.'

'Or Australia, or Timbuktu, or the North Pole, or Mars. I don't care where I live, as long as I'm with you. I love you, Immi.'

Her eyes were pure gold. 'I love you, too, Matt. You've helped me to accept myself for who I am. And with you by my side I have the courage to reach for my dreams. It wasn't supposed to happen. I wasn't meant to fall in love with you. We were supposed to be just helping each other through a crossroads.'

'Maybe we have,' he said. 'Because you showed me what I want in life. I want a partner, someone who'll watch the sunset and the stars with me, who'll be there to share the good times and the less good times. But I want that partner to be you.'

'There was a time,' she said, 'when I would've questioned if I would be enough for you. But the way you make me feel—I know I'm enough.' She kissed him. 'I love you, too. But I don't want you to miss out on travelling.'

'Come with me,' he said. 'And I was thinking: I quite like the idea of a trip to Northern Europe. Going to see the polar bears and the whales—especially if a small plane's involved and I'm on honeymoon with the pilot.'

'What about Hawaii and the solar telescope you wanted to see?'

'We can do that, too. We don't have to follow anyone's rules on a honeymoon, Immi. We can do whatever we like. Same as the wedding.'

'I definitely don't want a big glitzy affair like the one I planned with Stephen,' she said. 'Though I don't want to go quite as far as Portia and elope.'

'Then we'll go for something simple. We'll invite your family and mine, our closest friends and colleagues, to share the joy of the day with us. And we'll work out the details whenever,' he said. 'The dress, the food, the location—none of it's important. It's making those promises to each other that count. To love, honour and cherish.'

'To love, honour and cherish,' she echoed. 'To share our lives.'

'I love you, Imogen Marlowe,' he said softly. 'Be my moon and stars.'

'I love you, Matthew Stark,' she said, and kissed him. 'Be the wind beneath my wings.'

'Always,' he said. *Always.*

EPILOGUE

Three days later

'I CAN'T BELIEVE you gave us just three days' notice,' Andie said. '*Three days*, Immi. How were we all supposed to muck in and help?'

'It's fine,' Immi soothed. 'And there wasn't that much to do.'

'For your engagement party?' Portia asked.

'Hey—you eloped, so you don't get to nag me over this,' Immi said with a grin. 'It's fine, Portia. Matt helped me—it wasn't like when Stephen left me to organise everything.'

'And the fact you let him help says a lot about him,' Andie added.

'What do you really need for an engagement party anyway?' Immi asked. 'The most important thing is the people, and you're all here—the three of you, Cleve and Javier, Mum and Dad, Matt's mum and Matt's sisters.'

'An engagement party means food, wine, and music,' Portia reminded her. 'Somewhere glitzy.'

'Matt's sorted out the music, Gloria and her friend Giovanna talked Carlo into delivering the food and wine, and I happen to think that the garden of the Villa Rosa is the most perfect place for a party,' Immi said.

'It looks amazing,' Posy said. 'I can't believe how much you've done to it, Immi. It's so different.'

'All I did was cut back the shrubs, use the chippings as mulch, and plant a few pots. And it's all low-maintenance, so you don't have to worry about hiring a gardener to keep it up,' Immi said. 'Oh, and the fairy lights were Matt's idea. They're solar powered. He says if you hate them you can just get rid of them.'

'Fairy lights out here at night would be awesome,' Andie said. 'But, still. Three days, Immi.'

'We didn't want to wait. We wanted the rest of our lives to start now,' Immi said simply.

'And we all love you enough to come here. Though Dad took one look at the villa and insisted on booking a hotel for him and Mum,' Portia said wryly. 'He couldn't quite handle slumming it with his daughters.'

'The villa isn't a slum. It just needs a little more TLC,' Andie protested. 'Posy, don't listen to anything Dad says. Portia, you and I will get Javier and Cleve to stand either side of Dad and make him shut up when he starts to say something tactless, OK?'

'Good plan,' Portia said.

'Matt's sisters and brothers-in-law are all staying with Gloria tonight,' Immi said.

'So where are you and Matt staying tonight?' Posy asked.

'I don't know. He won't tell me.' Immi grinned. 'But I do know one thing. Wherever it is, it'll have an amazing view of the stars.'

'So are you staying here on the island?' Portia asked.

'No. We've talked it through with Mum, Dad and Gloria, and we're going to live in Cambridge,' Immi explained. 'We're getting a house with a granny annexe, so Gloria can live with us in the summer but keep her independence. I'm going to take a flight instructor course and work part-time as an instructor and part-time as Dad's test pilot, and Matt's going to university to study astrophysics.' She smiled. 'It's weird. I came here a month ago with my life in shreds and no idea what I was going to do—and then I met Matt and everything changed.'

'I'm glad,' Posy said. 'It's good to see you happy.'

'And Matt's a nice guy. I never liked Slimy Stephen,' Andie said.

'Agreed,' Portia chimed in. 'I could never put my finger on it, but there was something untrustworthy about him. Unlike Matt.'

'I know it all happened crazily fast,' Immi said,

'but it just feels right. I look at him the way you look at Cleve, Andie—the way you look at Javier, Portia. As if he's my moon and stars together.'

'If you're happy, we're happy,' Andie said.

'So I guess we get to borrow dresses from Sofia again,' Posy said. 'Which kind of keeps her with us at the party.'

'And Gloria,' Immi said, 'will no doubt be persuading everyone to drink Negronis on Sofia's behalf.'

Andie hugged her. 'I need an alcohol-free version. Don't you dare get married to Matt until after I've had the baby, so I can toast you properly in bubbles instead of having just one sip.'

Immi hugged her twin back. 'Deal,' she said.

'Let's get ready,' Posy said. 'And Matt's not going to believe his eyes when he sees you.'

Immi smiled. 'He says he doesn't care if I come to the party wearing my scruffiest cut-off jeans and a raggy old sweatshirt.'

Andie hooted. 'And this from the queen of power suits. Hasn't he seen you in work mode?'

'Yes. But he's right,' Immi said softly. 'The only thing that matters is having our family with us tonight. Everything else is just trappings.'

Andie and Portia looked gooey-eyed at that, as only newlyweds could, and Posy looked slightly sad. Immi hugged her. 'Hey. If you need to talk, you know I'm always here for you,' she said, keeping her voice low. 'You're my little sister and I love you.'

'Love you, too.' Posy's voice was slightly wobbly.

'Let's go and get ready,' Immi said softly.

At sunset, everyone arrived for the party. Matt had rigged up some extra strands of fairy lights, Javier and Cleve had set up a table in the conservatory for the food and wine, and Matt had sorted out a sound system.

'OK?' Matt asked. 'We don't have to do this if you don't want to.'

'I want to,' Immi said. 'Because I love you, and I want the whole world to know.'

He stole a kiss. 'I just smudged your make-up.'

She grinned. 'Trappings. And you could've worn the most clashing Hawaiian shirt and board shorts instead of that suit.'

'You could've worn your filthiest gardening gear,' he countered. 'Nothing matters, as long as we're together.'

'So are you going to tell me where we're staying tonight?' she asked.

'Nope.' He stroked her face. 'But I'm going to wake with you in my arms tomorrow morning.' And the love in his eyes made her knees feel weak.

'That's good enough for me,' she said.

'Let's get this party going,' he said, and drew her over to the centre of the terrace.

'Good evening, everyone,' Matt said.

There was a general chorus of 'good evening'.

'We're going to start with the speech, because we know we can't get out of it,' Matt said, 'and then I want everyone to party and enjoy themselves. My mum's made Negronis in honour of Sofia, so please charge your glasses because I want to make a toast to my fiancée.'

His words were greeted with general applause.

'Immi and I met when we were both at a crossroads,' Matt continued. 'We talked—more than I've ever talked to anyone in my entire life.'

'You talk too much anyway,' Gloria called.

'So does Immi—because she's a Marlowe girl,' Andie teased.

'She certainly is—and the Marlowe girls are amazing.' Matt smiled back. 'So we talked. Quite a bit. And then we discovered that the way forward from the crossroads, for both of us, was together. Immi's everything I want. She's clever, she's brave, she's amazing behind the controls of a plane—and she's also the most beautiful woman I've ever met. Every day when I'm with her, it could be raining and it'd feel as if the sun was shining because she's by my side.'

He dropped to one knee in front of Immi and

held up the pretty diamond and tanzanite ring they'd picked out together in Cambridge before flying back to the island to arrange their engagement party. 'Imogen Marlowe, I love you with every atom of my being. Will you marry me?'

'Matthew Stark, I love you, too. Yes,' she said, and he slid the ring onto her finger.

Then Matt got to his feet in one lithe movement, pulled her into his arms, and kissed her soundly—to the applause and whooping of their entire family.

'To my fiancée,' Matt said. 'My moon and stars.'

'To my fiancé,' Immi said, not to be outdone. 'The wind beneath my wings.'

'Let the party begin,' he said. 'And may tonight be as happy as the rest of our lives.'

Immi smiled at him. 'I love you. And you are, you know.'

'Just as you are for me,' he said softly.

* * * * *

If you really loved this story then don't miss
HIS SHY CINDERELLA
by Kate Hardy.
Available now!

If you enjoyed this story and can't wait to read
the next Mediterranean romance in the
SUMMER AT VILLA ROSA *quartet,*
the fourth and final book,
A PROPOSAL FROM THE CROWN PRINCE
by Jessica Gilmore, is out next month!

MILLS & BOON®
Large Print – December 2017

An Heir Made in the Marriage Bed
Anne Mather

The Prince's Stolen Virgin
Maisey Yates

Protecting His Defiant Innocent
Michelle Smart

Pregnant at Acosta's Demand
Maya Blake

The Secret He Must Claim
Chantelle Shaw

Carrying the Spaniard's Child
Jennie Lucas

A Ring for the Greek's Baby
Melanie Milburne

The Runaway Bride and the Billionaire
Kate Hardy

The Boss's Fake Fiancée
Susan Meier

The Millionaire's Redemption
Therese Beharrie

Captivated by the Enigmatic Tycoon
Bella Bucannon